THE CENTIPEDES

GW00746018

PIYUSH SRIVASTAVA

INDIA · SINGAPORE · MALAYSIA

Notion Press Media Pvt Ltd

No. 50, Chettiyar Agaram Main Road,
Vanagaram, Chennai, Tamil Nadu – 600 095

First Published by Notion Press 2021
Copyright © Piyush Srivastava 2021
All Rights Reserved.

ISBN 978-1-63850-530-3

DISCLAIMER

ONE

Humidity was high and perspiration soaked our clothes as my friends and I gathered in a dingy tavern in a congested, mysterious-looking alleyway in Paharganj, New Delhi. It was 9 p.m. We usually caught the last metro home.

The tapper knew us well. He knew that we were always in a hurry – feverishly rushing through the drinks. He sent out the bottles and plastic glasses within a minute of our arrival. We had no ritual to start guzzling. We wasted no time.

I allowed the whisky to trickle down my throat. I closed my eyes briefly and when I opened them again, I smiled.

I do not like the taste of alcohol. But over the years we, a group of five friends, had developed a habit of hanging around and sharing our experiences – both good and bad – while downing our drinks and wolfing down the peanuts or *papad*

This is my core group of friends. We don't care about festivals or holy days. Our drinking is not connected to religiosity or faith or even inhibitions. We normally don't burden ourselves with things that lead nowhere. Receptiveness is the key to getting together in our case.

It is not that we don't worship our gods. We believe that if something is bad, it is bad on any day of the week or month or season. And if it is not taboo for a moment then it cannot be taboo ever.

Maybe, we formed this view for our convenience. But then there is no denying that we stick to it religiously throughout the year.

As we cannot remain silent while drinking, we discuss random stuff just for the sake of it. Our discussions range from the new woman in the office to patriotism, which is the hottest topic in both the first and the third world – America and our country. In the past few months, a political party had almost proved that patriotism and supporting it were synonymous. Our country was now divided into two kinds of people – the patriots, who supported the political party and the unpatriotic, who did not.

Thankfully, there are still people who do not mind being branded traitors. They know that this particular political dispensation is taking the country to hell, consciously and systematically.

The loyalty of this political party lies with a few select corporate houses. These houses control the country's data and release information selectively.

Patriotism, for them, means standing by their mischief; standing by them even when they kill someone for being from a certain religion or caste that doesn't suit them politically or socially.

If you speak of the poor or those who died from hunger, a victim of gang-raping who immolated herself in shame, the rising prices of potato and onion, potholes on the roads, absence of teachers in schools or the lynching of a Muslim or a Christian; you will be attacked from all sides, dubbed a traitor, an anti-national, defaming the concept of the New India.

Their supporters are forthcoming when talking about the national flag and equally enthusiastic when debating as to why the minorities should not follow the civil norms of the majority community.

For example, making mandatory the seven rounds around the fire before a marriage is solemnised and the couple declared man and wife.

Those who question them are made to feel that they are from an enemy country, not authorised to question the new concept of exclusivity in India.

Their coming to power was inevitable because their main rival, an old political party, the torchbearer of anarchy in the country, showed complete disregard for public opinion on any issue. Their leaders misbehaved with the people and minted money through all possible sources. The leaders of this corrupt old party believed, through their elitist arrogance, that the power earned over the decades qualified them to run the nation or the government, that power was their right in perpetuity. They did not realise that the public had developed such a distaste for them that they would vote for even a guttersnipe the next time around just to keep them out of power.

The only difference between the old party and the emerging one was that the first didn't apply the term "anti-national" to their critics.

The five of us disapproved of both – the old party that kept insulting the people as well as the sub-continent for years and the new party that was systematically spreading political or ideological misinformation or contaminated knowledge with the help of its many wings. Like the desperate movement of a centipede in the gutter.

We were unanimous in our belief that the one in power and the one that was to come to power, and the people who were willing to be with either of the two, were ultimately the arms and legs of the same centipede.

However, this was certainly not the best subject to discuss when we were drunk. The vibrant colours of the clothes of the leaders of the emerging party or their exclusively masculine, brute, illiterate speech or their unofficial spying on every Indian similar to what used to happen with the KGB in the Soviet Union, turned us off.

What we loved most were topics related to women. It was safe. It was about women and not sexuality. The subject was smooth and relaxing beyond doubt. Mixed with alcohol, it left an easing impact on our elements.

Why did the editor play up her weak story today? Is the editor-in-chief smoking excessively after his breakup with so and so? What did she have that he was reluctant to allow her to leave the organisation? Why didn't she register a police complaint against her editor earlier? After all, he had been touching her inappropriately in the lift for the past year. What made her do so now?

This is how we would unburden ourselves at the end of a hectic, tiring and sometimes frustrating day. We never needed any other kind of entertainment.

Today, we were discussing the problem one of us – from the advertisement department – was facing.

He had gone to attend the funeral of a college mate's father. The Principal Secretary of State for Information and Publicity was also there.

My friend arrived at work two hours late because of this. His boss enquired about his late arrival and asked, "What happened to the special supplement you were assigned to do next week?"

"Sir, I am trying for it," he replied.

"No. You are not trying for it. I heard that the principal secretary was also there at the funeral. You should have talked to him about it there because he is not available in his office most of the time."

The boss wanted him to talk to the bureaucrat about releasing state government advertisements for the newspaper when the last rites were going on. After all, 70 percent of the newspaper comprises of government advertisements.

Being insensitive while employed in one of the most sensible trades is not new. It is like the politicians' coldness. If they announce a welfare plan for the poor, there is every possibility that they are going to snatch something from the poor. When they say they are going to strengthen the economy of the country, then you must be prepared for an artificial economic depression. When they say your money is safe in the bank then the people should start worrying. The virus of politics has entered most minds.

Harbouring socio-politico-criminal intentions and thinking the worst of any situation is a new fad, practised by the political class. And they are an inspiration to many.

An editor in a previous organisation while in the presence of two other editors promised to promote me at the time of my annual appraisal. But a few months on, he suffered a massive heart attack and passed away.

I reminded the editor present about the promise. He said: "Very well, the doors of hell are open to you. Please go there and ask for the promotion from the one who is there waiting for you."

We are resentful of our present or previous bosses but cannot do anything about it because most of them are heads of one or the other verticals of the groups and so enjoy unlimited power because of their proximity with the proprietors or their daughters or his/her secretaries or drivers.

TWO

●●●●●●●●●●●⋯⋯⋯⋯⋯⋯●●●●●●●●●●●

O ccasionally, a dozen or more friends join us. Some of them don't drink during Navratri because they consider it a sin. A few others do not drink during the month of Ramadan.

There was a time when I would argue with them.

"How could something be sinful for nine days and good for the rest of the year? Can something be dirty for a month and become consumable during the remaining eleven months?"

But, of late, I have realised that it is a futile argument that leads only to bitterness. I have lost many friends over such squabbles. Now we don't talk to each other even when we are sitting in the same coach of the metro, even if we happen to be sitting side-by-side. Previously, we used to share the same cigarette.

Now I believe that an argument over any issue is a bad idea.

Earlier, some friends would launch the conversation with the brand of liquor and gradually reach the latest political act or plan of a government or a political party. That used to be a deadly point.

It always ended up with everyone being in a bad mood.

"What is your politics?"

"What is your politics?"

"You are a bloody leftist."

"You are a stupid rightist."

The quickest way to lose a friend is to make public your political or social ideologies.

In the past, two of my friends were so angry with me because I questioned a state government of intentionally killing a person of a religious minority in the name of alleged involvement in terrorist activities. They sent anonymous letters to the proprietor of my newspaper and intelligence agencies, claiming that I was hand-in-glove with anti-nationals.

One day, one of them openly shouted at me and used foul language against my mother, sister and me. I threw a glass of water on his face and left.

A few months later, I came to know that he was a member of an extreme right-wing social organisation that boasted of its political clout. Among its achievements was the successful killing of the greatest leader of the country. At the same time, they claimed the legacy of the assassinated leader.

My former friend was prone to using the most objectionable words against anybody who did not subscribe to his ideology. His victim may not be able to forget it the next day but he would shake hands and smile as if nothing had happened. Maybe he would repeat the act in the evening.

Our present group of friends knew we had to pick a subject on which we had the same view. That way there would be no bitterness at the end of the day, even if we briefly discussed patriotism.

THREE

●●●●●●●●●●················●●●●●●●

The little knowledge I gained from newspapers about medical science makes me believe that although a normal prostate gland of a person of my age should be 25 grams, mine is only 14 grams. As a result, I need to go to the washroom more often than my friends. And, I am in the habit of topping 60 ml of whisky with water.

The drink works quickly on my mind and my bladder.

I walked into the restroom, which was full of people. It was bereft of faucets. A small green bulb illuminated the space. I screwed up my eyes to see the faces.

I held my breath because the smell of urine was strong and pungent.

There was graffiti on the walls of the restroom, alongside Hindi couplets on sex and sexuality.

Such writings are popular in the toilets of our trains too. It is called 'loo literature'.

Suddenly I felt someone behind me. When I turn around, a voice greeted me:

"How are you, sir?"

I didn't answer.

"What is the time, sir?"

The way he said 'sir' was different.

He was saying "saar".

I saw a round-faced, fair-complexioned man in his early 30s, almost my height. He was standing in front of me. My friends say I speak softly. But his voice was softer than mine and he was smiling.

"It is 9:30 PM," I replied, looking at my old wristwatch, the one my father gifted me.

"What are you reading on the wall, sir?" he asked me. "Read this. I have drawn this and written this poem," he said pointing to his creative work on the wall.

"You are a good poet," I said sarcastically without looking to his right, where the said art was displayed. He thought I was appreciating his work.

"Let me know if anybody in Delhi bothers you, sir. I will pump bullets in his head." He lifted his white shirt a little and showed me a pistol pushed into his waistband.

I was amused as well as frightened. I knew many people in the town who committed crimes for fun but never was such an offer made.

"I am saying this seriously," he said, his voice muffled.

Although he was drunk and unable to open his eyes properly, his eyeballs were moving like a pendulum as if scanning my face and mind.

"I'll let you know," I replied. "By the way..."

"You must," he interjected and walked away.

I came out of the loo, gasping for fresh air and almost ran towards the table where my friends were sitting. There was a sense of security there at that table. I didn't tell them about the dopey man I encountered in the worst place in the world, which I visited more frequently than others.

I picked up my glass and got lost in the gossip of an intense affair going on between our editor and a woman, who was born a Hindu and later converted to Christianity. The latest was that she was planning to become a Muslim to marry the editor.

The editor in question was a club hopper. His new girlfriend was his companion in the clubs now. One friend narrated an interesting story.

"He wanted to introduce me to a source and asked me to meet him at the club at 3 pm yesterday. When I got there I saw him dancing with his girlfriend. He saw me and began walking towards me with his girlfriend in tow. A middle-aged man, holding the hand of a 19 or 20-year-old girl hollered at the editor and introduced her to him", my friend said quoting the middle-aged man as saying to the editor, "Meet my new wife."

"So what's funny about it?"

"Our editor's girlfriend is this man's previous wife."

"You mean the religion-hopping lady is that person's previous wife?"

We laughed and it was cathartic.

There were mostly desiccated faces in the pub. The transparent stickers from the bottle caps were strewn all over the place. Peanuts and onion slices were scattered on the floor.

Normally, I would run away from such a dirty place. But, I find it acceptable in a model liquor shop.

My attention fixed on a grey-haired man in a white khadi kurta and pyjama sitting with two men, both in their 40s and two women in their 20s. I presumed the women were Russian.

Eavesdropping on their conversation I understood that he was a Congress leader, recently defected from the party that pursued Hindu chauvinism. A rich man with poor purchasing power, he was there perhaps to entertain the Russian women.

The politician was boasting of his visit to Moscow when Mikhail Gorbachev was President of the Soviet Union and the general secretary of the Communist Party of the Soviet Union.

The khadi-clad man was drunk yet trying his best to impress the Russian women. I was unable to measure this rich man's political success level.

"I was the general secretary of my party. Gorbachev was the general secretary of his party. I called his office in the night and told his staff that a general secretary wanted to meet a general secretary. They were happy to hear this. They sent a Lamborghini for me. I met Gorbachev. I met him. I am telling you I met him."

He gave an extra emphasis on his last two sentences.

Then he turned to the Russian women, stared at one of them for about a minute, trying to read her expressionless face.

"I met him. I was his guest. You are my guest. My guest." The politician resumed his conversation while tapping his index finger on the right side of his nose.

"I have a farmhouse in Gurgaon. My men will take you there. You can stay there for weeks or even months. You are my guest. You can take money from me. You don't bother about anything. There is my party's government in Delhi and many states. My government. Everything is yours. I am also yours. All yours."

And, in a lower tone, he said, "And you are mine."

Then the politician opened his mouth expelling air, like a vacuum cleaner. I thought he was laughing in a friendly manner.

I knew that the meeting of a general secretary with a general secretary was a lie. He was like any other rightist or centrist politician.

His boastfulness reminded me of the story of George Farera, an Indian politician who began his career as a trade union leader. He wanted to become a union minister and in a few years, he succeeded.

On a visit to Tibet, Farera strayed over the border. The Chinese soldiers caught him and took him to their commander.

They did not understand Hindi or English, yet from his desperate explanation they understood that he was a 'great politician from India'. Four Chinese soldiers held him by his legs and hands and threw him back over the border.

On returning to New Delhi, he declared: "The situation along the Indo-Tibet border is grim and the Congress government is in a slumber."

I heard this story from Manohar Pant, a former union minister in a non-Congress government. He competed with the Tibet-returned politician.

A bureaucrat who had worked with both of them as Officer on Special Duty told me during a late-night party in a South Delhi hotel that besides the power tussle, the two rival politicians had one more reason to dislike each other – young Tibetan boys.

Success comes to a politician in India more easily than in other professions. Their success rate is over 90 per cent.

One day, you will find a politician standing at the door of another small politician and the next day he will be chief minister of the state.

A school dropout, turned concubine of a small-time movie director can suddenly become a powerful politician.

You can be a great politician here if you are not afraid of losing anything.

We have seen many such leaders who have reached the top. One day, they are nobodies in national politics and another day they hold important positions at the Centre.

This has happened more often with the rise of regionalism and the pride of caste in the country. After serving as slaves of the kings or the British Raj, a large section of the country has forgotten a liberated, dignified life. It is like the effect of nuclear weapons that can be seen even in future generations.

People are willing to die for a politician of their caste or region. They are happy when the politician insults them after giving them a few hundred or thousand rupees or finds employment for their children.

Although I loved sitting here, listening to the blather of the politician without making him conscious of my interest in him, my friends didn't have the time. Their wives had been calling them on their smartphones. One called her husband five or six times in the hour we were there, to warn him to stay within limits of the quota she had fixed for him or else she would lock the door and let him spend the night in the park in front of their apartment, as she had done a few months ago.

"It wouldn't be new for me. As you remember I have done this before. But at that time it was summer and not pre-winter," my friend quoted his wife threatening him, much to our delight.

Soon we dispersed – relaxed, happy and on time.

While looking for an auto-rickshaw to get to the metro station, I noticed the same man with a pistol, entering a cheap hotel with a middle-aged woman, her face caked with makeup. Careless and wigged out, he was unable to walk on his own. Or, perhaps he was pretending so that he could lean on the woman. She was smiling and helping him to walk.

Although I spent some time in Paharganj almost every day, I didn't know all the mysteries of this area. I had heard from one of my past editors that it was the best place for Thai food, erotic massages and suppressed fantasies.

But I was happiest after I had a few pegs in me. I didn't need anything thereafter to make me happy.

FOUR

●●●●●●●●●●●●●⋯⋯⋯⋯●●●●●●●●●

What may be exciting for others is monotonous for me. The next month was routine, though many things considered interesting in the world of politics, society and entertainment continued to make news.

As a roving correspondent, I get to meet several people in Delhi and Uttar Pradesh every month for my stories or just for expert comment or simply to enrich my knowledge. This month I met a Hindi writer, a rapist, a victim, politicians and professors, a sadhu and a disillusioned right-wing youth.

The writer was Doodhram, a retired reader of the University of Allahabad. He loved tickling the back of his female research scholars. He called them his admirers.

"I am like your father," he would say while allowing his fingers to stray on their back without fear of being charged with sexual harassment.

I had heard he had deserted his first wife because she was a rustic, uneducated woman. His second wife was a television artiste.

Besides touching his female students, Doodhram loved spending time in the houses of his friends who had young daughters.

He had written many stories. One of his stories was a detailed description of his wife sitting in a Turkish style toilet without a door. His most recent story was his fantasies with the eldest daughter of one of his poet friends.

The author was of the view that a reader of Hindi literature lacked the depth to understand the essence of his writing.

"You are an English journalist. I know you will understand me and my writings better. I can be likened to Ernest Hemingway. You can write all this about me," suggested Doodhram without confirming if I wanted to write about him.

If a journalist meets someone who is not his family member or friend, then it is presumed he is going to write about them.

The writer also claimed that Gabriel Garcia Marquez in his *One Hundred Years of Solitude* was influenced by one of his stories written in the early 1960s.

One day, sitting on his lawn, my eyes fell on lingerie hanging on a clothesline. He noticed me looking at the colourful bits and pieces and chortled with glee, his teeth shining: "My daughter's clothes."

He realised from the expression on my face that I was surprised.

"You are an English journalist. That is why I am frank with you. Hindi people are narrow-minded," he said.

That was the first time I realised that as I was an English journalist, I was not a narrow-minded person. I wanted to look at myself in a mirror. I didn't have one with me to satisfy me at once.

Doodhram was a member of the communist party. He confessed that he didn't mind touching the feet of the senior leaders of the right-wing party or the Tibet-returned politician's competitor, Manohar Pant.

Then there was Ashutosh Singh, a 26-year-old youth from an affluent political family in Lucknow who had sexually assaulted a girl when she was 12 years old. With the help of the officers of the education department, his lawyers forged his documents and tried to prove in the lower court that he was a minor at the time of the crime. But a few social groups came forward to fight the legal battle for the victim who belonged to a poor family. Her father was a driver of the state bus service

The higher court ruled that Ashutosh was a major when he had raped the girl and awarded him seven years in prison. Within a year of his jail term, he was shifted to a hospital on health grounds. Almost every day, Ashutosh called the girl from different cell numbers and threatened her to expect worse if she did not stop making statements to the media against him.

The rapist was preparing to contest in the next election on a socialist party's ticket. The leaders of the said party had recently declared that rape was not a heinous crime and the perpetrator of the crime be treated sympathetically.

"I want to be chief minister and do social work to wash off my sins," said Ashutosh, when he met me.

The first wife of the leader of the socialist party, who agreed to give Ashutosh a ticket, had lost her mental balance when she discovered that her husband, Mausam Yadav, had another wife. She spent the last eight years of her life in a room in their home in their village, which was converted into a mental asylum.

Mausam sent his son to a distant city and then to Canada to study and stay away from his mother.

The rape victim, on the other hand, said that she had learnt in the course of her five-year court battle that the man would terrorise her all her life.

"He may kill me someday. But, often I don't feel alive. What is there to fear him?"

One politician I met, wanted to become the Prime Minister of India. Bhanu Mati was a stone-faced woman who had recently inducted a local heavyweight into her party. A few years ago, she had registered a case against him, for attempted rape.

"He locked me in a room, tore off my *kurta* and tried to outrage my modesty," she stated in her handwritten complaint to the police.

The 'stone-face' believed she could easily become Prime Minister if she had money to buy the Members of Parliament of other parties. And, Bhanu Mati was collecting it from all possible sources every day.

"I have a vote-bank for you. What do you have for me?" This was Bhanu Mati's standard question to whoever met her for a party ticket to contest an election.

There were only two answers to impress her.

One: "Money."

Two: "I am ready to give you whatever you ask for."

Bhanu Mati was also heard telling members of her party that she was a goddess and they should offer her diamond and gold in return for her blessings.

Once she asked the trusted general secretary of her party to hire a killer to eliminate a reporter who had broken a story about her taking possession of state-owned lands for her son. The reporter got wind of her plan and ran away from the city for two months. She then gifted the editor of the newspaper, where the said reporter was working, two prime plots of land on condition that the reporter would be sacked.

The editor was known for his courageous journalism. He called the reporter to his office and handed him his letter of suspension on disciplinary grounds saying, "You filed a lousy story against the politician. You forget that we maintain the highest standards of journalism."

"I am only the writer of the story. It was you who decided to publish it on the front page," said the reporter.

"You are arguing with me!" The editor stood up and said, "Goodbye."

Another politician I met during those monotonous days had recently created a flutter alleging that his cook was a member of a terrorist organisation and had tried to poison him. The cook, a forward caste Hindu, was arrested and jailed.

Later, I came to know from an aide of Pahar Joshi, the politician, the actual reason behind his anger. His cook knew that Joshi's daughter was having an affair with the boy next door and had not alerted him. Joshi scratched the cook's face before handing him over to the police.

The politician, an elected member of a House, had also scratched his daughter's face for falling in love with a man from a different caste.

He was referred to as *muh nochwa neta* (face-scratcher politician), by some of his followers in their private conversations. I met him for the second time in three days, in his house. He walked towards me. I realised (maybe I was wrong) that there was anger in his eyes and I ran towards the gate to protect my face.

But, the most interesting politician I met was Abdul Dolly, a leader once close to Sanoj Kumar, the son of a former chief minister. There are stories of Sanoj and Dolly kidnapping girls for their pleasure and disposing of them. Later, Dolly married a film actor.

One evening, I met Dolly in his lush, green farmhouse. He offered me a drink. I inadvertently asked him about his love affair with the actor. There was a sudden remarkable glow on his face. He immediately called his six security men who were also his henchmen. Then he raised his voice and chanted: "Reshma *ki chuchi* (the nipples of Reshma)."

His security men completed the slogan: "*Himalaya se unchi* (Taller than the Himalayas)."

Reshma was the actor he had married. She was at home. She heard the slogan, came out and sat with us, a delicate smile playing on her face.

Dolly had exercised great power during the days of his friendship with the former chief minister's son. But he was deprived of that unchecked power now. This was the reason he was bored and offered me a drink, and of course, chanted slogans in honour of his wife.

Boredom causes many to break private, social and legal boundaries. Some people drink, write, make love or kill while others rape an individual or an entire society.

I also met Arjun Kulkarni, a professor at the Indian Institute of Technology. He was a middle-aged man. He would gather a large number of students on the grounds of the institute and lecture them on patriotism. Recently, one of his students died when a bomb he was manufacturing accidentally went off.

This professor of engineering told me that his student was a nationalist and patriot.

"He wanted to correct the mistakes committed by the founders of the nation. He was a hero."

"I am an artist and can produce or shape more such heroes."

I asked Kulkarni about his family and he said, "My daughter is an engineer and has settled in Australia. My son is studying management at an institute in Illinois. They have no plans of returning to India."

It reminded me of a popular saying in India about wanting Bhagat Singh to be born again. But he should be born in the neighbour's family. Bhagat Singh was a legendary revolutionary freedom fighter. He was hanged to death during British rule.

Shyamanand, the sadhu I met, was in his late 30s. He had run away to Kanpur, from his ashram in Delhi when a woman registered a case against him for forcing her into the flesh trade. The police were not able to find him. With the help of a disciple, I met him in his hideout. There were two Members of Parliament sitting at his feet when I entered the hall. He was sunk in a magnificently decorated sofa.

"I am innocent. This woman who filed a police complaint against me is a blackmailer and a prostitute. She wants money from me." He had a mellifluous voice.

He spoke like he was singing.

Shyamanand got up, pushed play on a tape recorder that was on a small table near his sofa and began dancing. It was an Indian snake dance. The song was from an old Hindi movie in which the snake charmer falls in love with the snake.

Wrapped in a milky-white single cloth, Shyamanand would double up with laughter at regular intervals.

I was feeling suffocated and wanted to leave. But he signalled to me with a movement of his left hand to sit. After a while, one of the Parliamentarians also started dancing with him.

I didn't know whether he noticed the disdainful grimace on my face. I stayed there for about an hour, watching his dance.

Some teenage girls, who perhaps belonged to the house, were watching Shyamanand from behind a door left ajar trying to suppress their laughter.

The sadhu allowed me to leave only when his disciple, the owner of the house, brought fresh potato chips, which he offered to me as *prasad*.

"You must keep it for seven days and eat it every morning. All your wishes would be heard by the almighty."

"Write a good report about me and I promise you, you will soon become an editor."

Later, an officer of the intelligence bureau told me that a large number of respected sadhus had unsuccessfully lobbied to declare Shyamanand a Shankaracharya.

He was also involved in several bomb blasts in the country. But people believed that the government was afraid to lay a hand on him because a majority of voters would be annoyed.

Certain reports said Shyamanand had used a cell phone to trigger a blast in a shrine. The idea was to provoke two communities to clash. He had succeeded in his plan as six people had died in communal violence. His movement between Vidarbha and east Uttar Pradesh was frequent. I didn't know much about the incident except what had appeared in newspapers.

The right-wing political organisations were continuously issuing statements in his support.

Raju Misir, the disillusioned youth whom I met had lost his mental balance when a temple was not constructed in an east Uttar Pradesh town in early 2000.

He had been an active member of an organisation, which was pushing for it. Originally from the cow belt, he was deployed in Assam to change the perception of the people towards the organisation.

He gifted a Tulsi plant to every household in Assam saying: "Our mothers, sisters, wives and daughters worship the Tulsi. It is a medicinal plant for you. We both use Tulsi."

This was how Raju initiated a conversation with them before narrating 'the social work' he and his friends were doing in the region. Many times he contracted malarial fever. He came back to Uttar Pradesh to be a part of a crowd that razed a mosque.

Before this, terrorism was confined to Jammu and Kashmir and the northeast states. Now, it had the entire country into its grip.

The Muslims in this country, who felt secure in their religiosity, were suddenly afraid after these developments.

All of us know that insecure people can turn violent.

Raju was so eager to bring his party to power that he bought a serpent from a snake charmer and threw it on the leader of a rival party while he was addressing a rally. He was beaten up by the supporters of the politician and left to bleed. Raju was in a coma for three days.

Then, one morning, people saw him banging his head against a stone.

He spent four years in a mental asylum. Later, some of his friends made him the priest of a small temple where he used to do puja every morning and evening. He would seek God's blessings to give him enough strength to build a magnificent temple there.

FIVE

●●●●●●●●●●··············●●●●●●●●●●

I had met a cross-section of people. However, the next couple of weeks passed without a good or relevant story in hand. Such a situation created in me professional insecurity and tension.

I am in the habit of constantly chasing human-interest stories with a political angle. That is the only thing that brings a good increment at the end of the financial year. Otherwise, my EMI would exceed my salary, forcing me to sell my flat or car.

There is always a sense of professional insecurity in me. And, it gets worse when I have no story to write.

Fortunately, my editor has never imposed a time frame on my stories. All the same, I cannot stop thinking that I may be punished soon.

He might think I am a lazy reporter. Maybe he is waiting for the end of the year to spoil my annual appraisal. Maybe he will transfer me to a less important location, where I have to rent a house and develop new contacts.

Such thoughts give me nightmares.

During these story-less days, I asked my colleagues a hundred times whether the editor had said or asked about me.

My colleagues would reply that he had said nothing. I was not satisfied. Who knows? Maybe a colleague is harbouring an ambition to replace me?

Every morning, I send messages to my editor.

"Today's edition is great. People in my apartment appreciated it."

"You have written a great edit. The Human Resource Development minister was praising it."

Mostly, I lied to initiate a conversation with him. But his answers were monosyllabic:

"Thanks."

"OK."

His single word replies would enhance my worries.

With time I was disillusioned.

SIX

• • • • • • • • • •••••••••••••• • • • • • •

A girl was brutally raped by some men in Delhi. Four days after the incident, my boss called me up early in the morning. I was still in bed.

The undergraduate student was going back home with her boyfriend after watching a late-night movie when the incident took place.

The editor asked me to rush to the girl's village in Bhadohi district of east Uttar Pradesh where she was born. It was like a rebirth for me, at least in my imagination.

After a month of enforced idleness, I did not know where to anchor myself in this cutthroat world.

An assignment means everything is fine with me in the office and I am still there.

"Good morning! How are you?"

"I am fine, thank you!"

I asked myself and replied as I jumped out of bed happily.

The government had given the victim's family a compensation of Rs 20 lakh and an air ticket to fly to Varanasi, the nearest airport to their village. They were supposed to perform rituals at the ancestral place of the brutalised soul.

After a hurried shower, I made tea for myself and called my acquaintance in Varanasi to know the details of the family.

I am known for having well-informed acquaintances in the districts. The reason is simple. Whenever I am away from Delhi, I invite local reporters to the hotel where I am staying, offer them drink and food with all the respect at my command. Elder or younger, I address them as *bhaiya* or 'sir' and listen to them attentively rather than expect them to listen to me when I speak. Occasionally when I lose interest in their conversation, I pretend I am listening to them with respect for their words.

The best thing about the reporters, in general, is that they start speaking too much too early. Alcohol fuels their words. Even I do that. But once out of Delhi, I keep my mouth shut.

It is also true that local reporters know more about the politicians and political trends than people like me sitting in Delhi and suffering from an Atlas Complex. They can tell you which minister demands exactly how much bribe for which work.

Who paid for an election ticket of a party, based as a champion of social justice?

Which coal-mafia from Dhanbad is funding the entire election campaign of which leader in east Uttar Pradesh?

Which party hopper politician has just found himself a new concubine in Uttarakhand?

Which minister in Allahabad, sleeping with a journalist-cum-socialite, was caught red-handed by his wife?

Which minister compared a woman to mythical nymphets in his love letter to a woman journalist? Why did he write: "You are my Menaka, you are my Urvashi."

Which woman politician, while being taught by her boyfriend to drive a car, met with an accident, and in an unconscious state mentioned his name?

Some of the more enterprising ones could tell you which intelligence bureau officer was courting which lady police inspector and which district magistrate was beaten up by his wife last night.

I am also lucky to have made friends among veteran provincial journalists.

Take for example Abrar Ahmad, who lives in Lucknow. He has been a silent spectator to the activities of a political dynasty for the last half-century.

I like spending time with him whenever I am there because he speaks with authority about the leaders of this family. However, what he loves the most is talking about Kaizaad Dhondi, the son-in-law of the family. Dhondi never liked his father-in-law, one of the greatest politicians of India.

As per the story narrated to me by Abrar, Kaizaad had become so powerful that he would ignore his father-in-law.

He had an extremely affectionate relationship with two aspiring women politicians and wanted to field them in the Assembly elections, according to my elderly friend.

The great leader of the political dynasty had assigned Chawdhary, a famous Jat leader of west Uttar Pradesh to select candidates for the party. Chawdhary told the great leader that his son-in-law was mounting pressure on him to field two "dubious but extremely pretty women" in the elections. It was decided after a marathon closed-door meeting that instead of creating a situation of confrontation within the family, they would call the two women and discourage them from joining electoral politics.

"You are so young and beautiful that you will not be able to survive in politics. You go home and get married and settle down with the handsome donation the party will arrange for you," Chawdhary told one of the women.

He called the other woman and said, "You look tender and cute. We have something better for you than an Assembly ticket. But first, you tell Kaizaad that you don't want to contest in the election."

The next day, Kaizaad rang up Chawdhary and said, "I am the family of the two women candidates and I have something much better for them than what you have in mind. Right now I want them to contest in the Assembly polls."

The nominations of both the women were announced within two hours.

No, this is not mere gossip. The veteran reporter could substantiate the information, which was never reported.

My acquaintance in Varanasi, Gaurav Pandey, a television reporter, excitedly told me on the phone that the rape victim's family had already reached Varanasi's Lal Bahadur Shastri International Airport.

"A central government officer was waiting for them with a hooter fitted luxury car to take them to their village in Bhadohi. We tried to talk to her father, Badreshwar Verma. But he appeared least interested in giving us soundbites," Gaurav said disappointedly when I called him again.

"An officer was also trying to keep us at bay with the help of the police", he said.

"I'll be there soon. I want to visit the village," I told Gaurav.

He was not sure whether my trip would be fruitful.

"The village is far from here and I don't think you will like travelling on such badly maintained roads," he warned me.

I reached the office an hour before the morning meeting. The guard at the reception was waiting for me.

"Ramayan sir, here is your ticket. I have informed Nahid that he has to accompany you. The editor wants a lot of close-ups."

We had tickets for the evening train. I had thought it would be a flight.

The editor came late and told me that he was expecting a human-interest angle to the stories and excellent pictures from Nahid.

I killed time by rewriting press releases knowing it wouldn't get any space in the newspaper.

When I arrived at the New Delhi Railway Station, the photographer was there. The train was on the platform. I got to work seconds after entering the coach. People were talking about the rape that had taken place. Some were agitated. Two of them were of the view that such incidents don't take place in Gujarat because there are strong-willed leaders. One of them said Uttar Pradesh and Bihar produced rapists.

I was trying to note down the quotes to give colour to my copy. I asked passengers, who seemed to be habitual and compulsive political commentators, their names and requested them to elaborate their views. They in turn asked me when their names would appear in the newspaper.

The train started on time from New Delhi but arrived in Varanasi six hours late.

We stayed for an hour in the waiting hall of the railway station and then hired a cab to take us to the village.

Gaurav was right. It was a tough journey by road – one that didn't exist at all. The driver was playing lewd Bhojpuri songs sung by a popular Bollywood singer, who had later become a Parliamentarian.

A survey conducted in Uttar Pradesh and Bihar in the late 1990s by a friend of mine who ran a music company found that people of this region loved watching and listening only to vulgar Bhojpuri films and songs.

"There is not a single Bhojpuri movie made in the last one year in which the hero and heroine don't meet in a sugarcane field and sing a song laden with sexual suggestions and imagery," the survey report said.

It was around 8:00 PM when we finally reached the village. The parents and brothers of the victim, Roshni Verma, had gone to sleep in their house, which looked big enough to accommodate five moderately-sized families. There were three big cowsheds, outside their ancestral house. The girl's uncle, Someshwar Verma was awake and smoking his hookah. He greeted us and offered us two rope cots to sleep on.

"You can stretch out here if you like," his voice stiff and uninviting.

Sleeping was not my priority. I was taking notes by the light of my mobile phone and questioning him.

Someshwar told me that Badreshwar discontinued his studies when he was in Class 10. Fifteen years ago, having inherited a small piece of agricultural land after its division among four brothers, he left the village and settled in the Laxmi Nagar area of Delhi.

He worked as a motor mechanic in a workshop and earned Rs 6000 a month.

"He went to Delhi to earn well and send his children to an English medium school. But he could never earn enough to realise his dream. So they studied in municipal schools," said Someshwar.

"We heard Kartik Tiwari, with whom Roshni went to watch a movie, studied in English medium." He yawned and left.

My photographer told me that there were some foreign journalists already camping there.

They were sleeping in the neighbouring rooms, which were cleaner than ours and had doors. While the temperature was around four degree Celsius, it was at least two degrees colder in our doorless room because of the humidity caused by cow dung and urine. There were brick walls only.

"Ask uncle if there is a hotel nearby," I told Nahid. I was not carrying a warm wrap.

"I already asked Someshwar. He said it is some 50 km from here and the roads are bad. I have two shawls. You take one." He gave me one, which barely covered the length of my body.

It was one of the longest nights of my life.

SEVEN

●●●●●●●●●●●●●●●●●●●●●●●●●●

I have been working in Delhi for the past 10 years and know the slums in the Laxmi Nagar area. The only VIP who visited once in many years was the local councillor of the Delhi Municipal Corporation. The stooges of the politicians can be seen there every evening standing near pan shops and treating the place as their office. They promise to get appointments for people to meet with one minister or the other to get their work done, in return for cash. Most of the people wanted to meet politicians for jobs for their children.

The man, whose daughter was raped, tortured and thrown out of a moving cab to die slowly and certainly, was suddenly very important for the most senior ministers and leaders of the country after an unprecedented protest against the law and order situation in the national capital.

People looked at the incident as a national tragedy, sorrow and shame. Foreign tourists were cancelling their visit to India. There was a general view that the country was unsafe to visit.

This at a time when many political dispensations claimed that they were all set to take India forward as a military superpower, an unbeatable world economy, a spiritual guru of the world.

Left parties said, the clumsy combination of ruling parties wanted to develop the country as a mental slum, where women were looked down upon and considered as objects.

Indian men were losing their online girlfriends from developed countries after this incident. Many youngsters had exchanged engagement rings online and were preparing to meet and get married. Some had already met their foreign girlfriends and agreed to tie the knot. They were instantly discarded by their cyber partners, girlfriends or fiancés, and for many youngsters, the dream of travelling abroad was shattered.

Several political leaders had met the parents of the gang-rape victim in the last few days and offered every support. They said they were pained by what had happened to Badreshwar's daughter. While most of them were in power at one stage or the other, none of them had anything honest or sincere to say. Instead, in front of media cameras, they blamed each other for the incident. Many of them compared their rivals to rapists. However, they could be seen moving in the Parliament and Assembly halls holding each other's hands.

The international and national media was instinctively or otherwise eager to give a new sensational turn to the story. I was looking for something different; I hoped to churn out something, which could make a lead story and prove my worth as a journalist.

My dreams were many, mostly unpleasant. In one dream, there was blood all over the street and someone in an expensive suit wearing diamond rings on all his fingers was covering it with currency notes.

I also saw in my sleep someone threatening me for having written a story against him. When I put down the phone and turned my face, I saw the man in the expensive suit standing behind me with a dozen of his henchmen. I tried to escape but my legs were fixed to the ground. Then suddenly I recognised the man's face. It was my father.

I asked him why he was doing this to me.

"Relationships are transparent," he answered and evaporated in the winter fog.

I knew that relationships were transparent. I had heard this before at a workshop organised by a theatre artist who was writing a play on the Bhopal gas tragedy of 1984. He had invited local people to narrate their experiences when everyone was running out of Bhopal to elude death.

"I was born in Bhopal and live here. My parents live on the other side of the city. When I heard that people were dying and the poisonous gas was spreading, I called my husband and asked him to take our two kids out of school and come home. We had to leave the city as quickly as possible."

"When we were five kms away from the city I remembered my parents and called them. They told me that they had already left Bhopal. They had not called me before running out of the city. And I didn't call them."

EIGHT

•••••••••••••••••••••••••••

When I woke up, I saw a reporter and his cameraperson standing in front of Badreshwar. I recognised him from the pictures in the newspapers and those shown on television channels. Sadly, it is against the law to show the faces of family members of a rape victim, even if she was dead.

The journalist in conversation with the father belonged to a news channel from the Middle East. Badreshwar was sitting on a jute cot on the lawn and answering his questions carefully and intelligently. His voice was balanced and his face was expressionless. He stood up suddenly, declaring that it was time for his breakfast. He perhaps knew nobody could afford to leave without interviewing him. A quality Badreshwar must have acquired, perhaps in the proximity of powerful people of India after the unfortunate incident with his daughter.

Nahid was waiting for me to wake up. He brought a mug of water for me to wash my face.

He takes good care of me. I am in the habit of being careless when on tour. I don't mind wearing crumpled clothes and flip-flops. I also don't comb my hair. It has also been my habit since my university days to sit on a bench at a roadside *dhaba* with my legs on either side.

During the previous elections, we were roaming in Bihar when Nahid got irritated with me because of this. I stopped a small-time politician near a *dhaba* while he was passing through during his campaign. We sat there for an hour and ate *samosas* with him. While leaving, the politician called me to a corner, gave me Rs 500 and said, "Please keep this for diesel in your car."

I returned the money to him politely and said, "Please don't worry about me. My company takes good care of me."

The politician was stunned at my behaviour.

"I pay reporters for interviewing me. They get angry if I don't gift them cash. They then write against me. I can pay you Rs 1000 if Rs 500 is too little. Please accept it and write only good things about me," he requested with his hands folded.

"I don't write good or bad about someone. I write only what I see and hear," I replied and backed off quickly.

Back in the car, Nahid asked me what the politician had said. I told him the story.

He was silent for 10 minutes and then exploded: "Sir, for god sake, please wear good clothes and shoes when you are travelling for stories. Or, I'll tell the editor that I will not accompany you the next time."

"Don't worry. I'll wear better clothes," I promised, to avoid any further conversation.

He had reason to complain. He was a tall man, who wore an expensive photographer's jacket and Ray-Ban sunglass even in the monsoon. He was a fashionable man, who had a beautiful wife and many girlfriends.

I never kept my promise of wearing ironed clothes and shined shoes. Even today, I am wearing jeans, a white round neck T-shirt, a heavy jacket and leather sandals.

I noticed that there was a pond in front of Badreshwar's ancestral whitewashed brick house – a sign of prosperity in such villages.

It was the last house in the village. There were agricultural lands spread over several acres on the other side of the pond. Three buffaloes, two oxen and a cow were tied on this side of the pond. There were also two granaries made of hay, husk and mud.

Over 50 villagers stood in different groups, talking in low voices. Some of them were staring at the television journalists with interest and curiosity.

Others were standing behind the father so that they too would be there in the frame of the cameras. One of them was continuously smiling mischievously and his right hand was on the shoulder of his fellow villager.

There were a dozen TV crew waiting for their turn.

NINE

●●●●●●●●●●············●●●●●●●●●●

Having no option, we waited our turn. I got the chance after one-and-a-half hours.

"Please be short and to the point," Badreshwar said in a carelessly detached voice.

"I am sorry as I am going to remind you of what you intend to forget." I apologised to him trying to be extra polite.

"You please start. I have interviews with some people from Britain and America." His voice was commanding and rough.

I realised that he was completely dissociated from my questions regarding his life and the life of his daughter or the incident that sparked an unexpected mass movement across the country. He was looking everywhere except at me while replying to my questions.

"All of us suffer in our lives. It happens." He summed up, even before I could start.

"The government is helpful too." I tried to grab his attention with my statement.

"Yes, the Prime Minister and the Chief Minister apologised to me for whatever happened in Delhi. They have promised me a better job and my elder son's admission to a good college. The CM talked to me on my mobile phone and told me to complete all the rituals and return to Delhi where another cheque of Rs 25 lakhs was kept for me," he said with a sense of pride.

"What was your daughter's dream? Did she ever share it with you?"

"She wanted to be a doctor and serve the nation. She was patriotic and wanted to help poor people."

"Whom do you hold responsible for the incident?"

He stared at me blankly for about 30 seconds and didn't utter a word.

Last night, while driving into the village I noticed that the roads were being repaired.

"Who is doing road repairs?" I asked him.

"The Chief Minister of Uttar Pradesh may come here to meet me. He called me yesterday and said that he would give me a cheque of Rs 15 lakh and also lay the foundation stone of a school here, to be named after my brave daughter. The district magistrate was here yesterday and told me that he has planned some development work here because my great daughter belonged to this village. This is the first time such things are happening in my village in my memory," he replied and then again stared at my face for about 10 seconds. This time he was expecting some reaction from me.

I saw a helipad being constructed and also a Swiss cottage at a distance from his house. I asked him about this.

"Don't you think politicians are trying to capitalise on this unfortunate incident?"

"After all he is Chief Minister of a state. He is an important person. Some arrangements should be made for him if he is coming here," said Badreshwar.

Meanwhile, Someshwar, who had been my host the previous night, interrupted us and informed his brother loudly that the local Member of Parliament was continuously calling him to know if he required anything.

The father didn't say anything but there was a glow on his face and a victorious smile that he couldn't control. I noticed he was hitting his left foot on the ground with musical frequency as if he was listening to a good song or music.

I asked him who the Member of Parliament was and he replied: "Manoj."

"Manoj?" I repeated with stress on "n".

"Yes," he answered as if the Parliamentarian was the boy next door.

"Ah, he is a marvellous person. I can call him on the phone. Maybe he is burdened with work. But despite that, he will come here whenever I call him."

"He is my dear man."

I spoke to Badreshwar in Hindi. But he used the words "marvellous" and "my dear" in English.

Both eyes were shining.

It was not the first time I was hearing the use of English words in a sentence. I was not surprised. But I didn't know that he knew a few words of English.

I have heard more interesting English words in a Hindi sentence before than the two the father uttered to me.

Once, while I was in Patna, I had gone to watch a movie starring Bollywood actor, Govinda, with my former girlfriend. While she was standing in the lady's queue, which was shorter than the men's queue, a man in his late 20s came to her and requested: "Sister, can you please buy my ticket also?" He said this in Hindi and then tried to give her money for the ticket. She refused.

The man came back again after five minutes and said: "Sister, please show mercy or I won't be able to watch this movie today." He used the word "mercy" in his Hindi sentence.

She didn't realise that he was trying to fit an English word he knew in his sentence, to convince her to buy his cinema ticket.

"No mercy," she replied angrily in English. "Go and die."

He looked at her blankly for a few seconds and left.

TEN

●●●●●●●●●●●⋯⋯⋯⋯●●●●●●●●●

Manoj was a lawmaker in one of the socialist parties of Central India. His father, a successful socialist politician, was a man who should be feared. His followers avoided inviting him for dinner to their homes.

An alumnus of the University of Allahabad, he survived on holding up travellers during his student days. He stole cash from passengers who got off the train at night and took a rickshaw to the main city area. He and his friends would apprehend such people near their hostel and sometimes even shoot them. Even as a student, he was popular in university and projected as prime ministerial material.

The prime ministerial material was already an alcoholic and a maniac by the time he emerged as a star in Indian politics. He would freely molest the women of his host's family. A large number of his admirers believed that he was a perfect politician.

Manoj belonged to the political party formed by Mahendra Jadhon, his father's disciple.

Claiming that he would fight for the rights of the backward class and minorities, Mahendra's entire family had become important in politics.

Mahendra's son, Bikas Jadhon, chief minister of a state for a time, hated his father. As a child, Bikas had seen his father torturing his mother. Mahendra had tried to poison his wife twice. She survived. He had many women in his life including Bollywood beauties. It was famously known that Mahendra preferred two 16-year-old girls to one woman of 30 or 32. Incidentally, a married woman who already had a son had video graphed his sexual adventures and blackmailed him into marrying her.

Mahendra's henchman wanted to eliminate the blackmailer but someone convinced him that he could get the vote of that particular caste if he married her.

Mahendra loved his son because he was his blood. The son had no love for his father because he knew of Mahendra's debauched lifestyle.

Mahendra married the blackmailer when his first wife was still alive. She died 13 years after his second marriage. The second wife, who was 15 years younger than him, had no problem with his debauchery. Her only concern was to establish her son from her first husband on a par with her stepson. She played super leader in Mahendra's house. She assigned two cabinet ministers in her stepson's ministry to give Rs 2 crore each to her son every month as pocket money.

She secretly assigned a practitioner of the black arts from Varanasi to conduct a round-the-clock ritual to change the position of the planets in her son's *kundali* so that he would become chief minister and also replace her second husband as president of the party.

Bikas believed his father was completely in the grip of his stepmother. I heard from close family sources that she had several video clips of her second husband with girls. Even Bikas knew about those video clips. He wished his stepmother would make those clips public. Bikas also harboured an ambition to become the president of the party and it was possible only when his father was finished politically.

Mahendra was not naïve. He trusted people in the party who would keep him posted about the activities of his son, his second wife, her son and daughter-in-law. At times, his informers would exaggerate the stories while narrating whatever had transpired.

Manoj was one of Bikas' trusted men. He pretended to be loyal to Mahendra's second wife. Every Monday, Manoj gave Bikas a report on the happenings in the family.

I had a complete plot for a soap opera on the drama of this party's first family and it had been playing in my mind in recent months.

ELEVEN

•••••••••••••••••••••••••••••

At that time, a man surrounded by four policemen arrived and broke my thought process. He was the district magistrate of Bhadohi.

"You don't worry about anything. I will manage everything. Let me know if you want to go anywhere. My car with a blue beacon will take you there. *Saheb* was telling me that you should tell the truth about the Delhi police to the media," the officer told Badreshwar and looked at me with disgust.

Then he dialled a number on his mobile phone, turned to the father and said, "*Saheb* wants to talk to you."

"*Kya agenda banae ho tum?* (What is your agenda?)" I could hear the voice on the other side as it happens on some phones if you are close by. It was a hard, confident but irritating voice.

"Sir," the father's voice choked. He wanted to say something but it was lost in his vocal cord.

"*Dekha kis tarah poora rashtra naraj hai? Tum Ma Bharati ke sapoot ho, yaad rahe* (Did you see how angry the entire nation is? Keep in mind that you are the son of Mother India.)"

The voice continued, "*Chahe koi kucch bhi de, isko rokne ke liye koi bayan mat dena. Main khayal rakh raha hun tumhara* (Don't try to stop all this, whatever they offer you. I am taking care of you.)"

The officer almost snatched the phone from the father and left as quickly as he had arrived.

"Some drunken people assaulted and brutalised your daughter for about an hour in a cab on the main roads of the national capital. There were no police to stop them," I tried to come back to the point I was on, before another interruption.

"The police did its job well." His voice was firm.

"What makes you think that the police did their job well? The police came onto the scene only when your daughter was almost dead."

"The police cannot provide security to every person in the country. I am satisfied that the police identified the criminals and arrested them within 24 hours. The Prime Minister met me. He was apologetic about whatever happened to my daughter. He has offered me security."

"Don't you think that the prevention of crime is an important aspect of governance?"

"Which newspaper did you say you work for?" He asked me instead of answering my query. His voice was still balanced. I told him the name of my newspaper.

"Is it a Delhi based newspaper?"

"It has 10 editions in India including one in Delhi."

"If you work for a good newspaper you should learn to ask relevant questions." Now his voice was stiff.

TWELVE

● ● ● ● ● ● ● ● ●····························● ● ● ● ● ● ● ● ●

Badreshwar's words were clothed in multiple political streams. He had no problem with the system, in fact by now he was very much a part of it or better to say he was quick to adjust to the contradictory political systems. He was fine with the existing dispensation and at the same time romancing with its critics and opponents. Effectively. Smartly.

I am sure, a few days ago, he had been a different man. He must have possessed the innocence of a poor rustic man, struggling against an unbearable day-to-day reality of life. But in the last few days, he had learnt something faster than expected. From nothingness to an upward-looking man. The father had acquired a rare quality to accept all and negate none, except people like me, who tried to see the restlessness in him... the restlessness of a common man.

A victim of the system converting tragedy into a grand national opportunity. The country mourned for his suffering and he accepted it as his birthright. Just a few days ago he might not have relished even his birth. Now, he was in the process of unlearning; learning to be as arrogant as the *nouveau riche* even before being rich; like a corrupt man newly appointed as a bureaucrat or a successful politician.

"What is the circulation of your newspaper?"

I was aghast. It is not that I don't face such questions. Once, an industrialist told me his driver preferred a particular newspaper to clean the windscreen of his car. He also told me that he paid the driver more than what I was being paid.

But people who ask these questions or behave in this manner are different. They are the special people of the Indian political and economic system. When they dislike a reporter they can be disgusting, say horrible things and ask uncomfortable questions. It is their way of insulting a reporter or reminding them that they are insignificant and the written word carries no weight. Power and money give the rich and powerful a chance to keep senior people in the newspaper industry in good humour. A reporter cannot harm them in any way.

In the present case, I knew well what to say to the father of the girl, who had unwittingly become the victim of monsters. Mine was a highly circulated newspaper. He might not have been aware of this because it was an English daily. I could be as rude because he was not yet one among those privileged people. With years of experience, I had learnt how to handle such subjects in their language.

But I had no wish to be harsh with Badreshwar. I was on an assignment to do human-interest stories and I wanted to do it with sensitivity. That was the only way to present the agony of this man to my readers, whom I considered intelligent.

I looked at him blankly. He realised that I was not willing to continue with this line of questioning as it defeated the very purpose of my tour.

My friends in the marketing division of the newspaper often tell me stories of their training while in college. I have heard from them that a manager shouldn't waste much of his or her time convincing the clients to place an order. They should be influenced at the first opportunity to get the work done as soon as possible.

This man could be the subject of a study for the marketing personnel. Besides, those who had made him like this in just a few days had not been trained to do so.

"This is the problem with Indian media," Badreshwar was gradually getting aggressive; more than I had ever experienced even with the most disgusting of politicians and businessmen.

"You must learn from these foreigners to frame a question," he said, pointing at two British women journalists.

I closed my eyes for about 10 seconds and tried my best to regain my composure. To a great extent, he had succeeded in insulting me. He had demoralised me. But I had to control my anger and other feelings.

One of my professors in university had once used foul words against me in the classroom. I asked him to keep his mouth shut or I would throw him from the second floor of the building. He never misbehaved with me again.

I have been aggressive in the past. I had attacked a religious leader on the campus just because he was speaking against a particular religion. There were many such examples in my life.

Today, I was in no mood to react abruptly. I had an assignment that could compensate for the many days of dullness I lived in, meeting interesting and not so interesting people.

I opened my eyes and said, "College and university students across the country, who don't see everything through a political mirror, are organising protests against the incident. They are taking out a candlelight march in the evening in cities and villages. Do you think that they should get back to their studies and forget about the gang-rape of your daughter?"

"Who are they protesting against?" He threw the question back at me, but quickly answered, "They are doing this to honour my daughter and to boost me and my family's morale. My daughter was their sister, their friend, their inspiration."

"I am satisfied with the role played by the governments. But the rapists should be hanged immediately, even if a new law is supposed to be enacted by this government. The people of the country are with me in demanding instant justice, be it on the street or in a court of law," he said.

I noticed an android phone in his hand with a picture of goddess Durga on its screen.

THIRTEEN

●●●●●●●●●●·····················●●●●●●●●●

That a rapist should be punished was something no one could deny. There may also be people who can advocate stoning a rapist to death.

I too believe that a rapist must be treated as a rogue animal. However, street justice has no space in any society.

What Badreshwar believed in was completely opposed to the view of the single-member panel, constituted by the government under retired judge, K. S. Sharma. People like me endorsed Sharma's honesty.

"Institutional apathy on the part of the ruling dispensation and failure of the law enforcing agencies are most important factors behind the growing confidence of the rapists," said Justice Sharma to the media in Delhi.

"The government's lack of sincerity towards the victims is the obvious root cause for the current unsafe environment that is eroding the rule of law. I am pained to see that the ruling class is still not showing any sign of regret for their mistakes. Some people dare to brutalise someone because they believe they can get away unpunished. The ruling dispensation and the lawmakers are busy blaming each other for the incident and capitalising on it," Sharma added, pointing out that similar incidents would happen repeatedly if the government did not send a strong message against the sexual assaulters.

"But no government or political party or authority will take responsibility to stop it. They behave as if it is part of their governance that rape should happen frequently in our society so that they can plan a political strategy around such an incident. We belong to a society which has a decades-old history of indifference towards the issues that affect the day-to-day life of the common man," Sharma further added.

Extremely modest and respectful towards all who met him, the retired judge was preparing his report without help or an office.

He converted one room of his two-bedroom flat in Noida into his office.

"Because the government has not given me an assistant or an office and I cannot afford a typist," Justice Sharma had laughed when a television reporter asked him about the government's apathy towards the work assigned to him.

Sharma was too polite to say that the politicians loved murderers and rapists. They needed the cruellest people as their workers to terrorise, extort and frighten the common man so that they would not dare to vote for their rivals, who could be equally cruel. Then some people from among them, mostly well connected but appearing impartial, would appeal to the voters to support whoever is less cruel, less criminal and less corrupt. Eventually, they will suggest to the voters the name of one who is less cruel than others.

Mahendra used to defend the rapists. Every time, such an incident took place he would say that it was a mistake committed by young men; they should be pardoned. I learnt that the politician had helped an officer of the Indian Police Services from Maharashtra charged in a rape case. The officer was about to be arrested when the politician stepped in and convinced the authorities to destroy the files against the top cop.

When the officer met Mahendra to say thank you, the leader said, "Be careful in future, when you want a woman under you against her wish. I may not be able to save you next time."

The politician and the officer belonged to the same caste and that was the only emotional bond between them. But who knows, maybe the act of rape is a stronger bond between two people.

I mention this police officer because he was part of many such teams, tasked to probe gang-rape cases in the past. He was called to Delhi when the brutal rape happened and asked to ensure that the public unrest was brought under control. Some believed it was this officer's idea to send the girl to the USA in the guise of treatment, though she had already been declared dead in an Indian hospital.

The political executives liked the idea and it gave them a chance to show citizens that they were sincere in trying to save the victim.

Knowing the potential of the officer, another political party in power in a state two years ago had picked him for a more ticklish job than anybody expected.

He was sent to Russia for training and then posted in Nasik for a month on a secret mission. Thereafter, he went on deputation to the Ministry of Defence. On returning to his cadre, he and his team rigged the election in favour of the party, which sent him to Russia.

Some rivals of the winning party believed that the officer's team could create an intense magnetic field around the voting machines and then use their Bluetooth to change data.

There was also a rumour that chips were installed in the pink paper used to wrap these machines. This was the most innovative idea to tamper with the voting machine. That was a skill par excellence and it was because of this that he could be saved from the timid and lewd hand of law enforcers even when he committed a rape or two. The technical experts always rejected this theory and ridiculed those who spread the rumour.

However, it was true that the said officer was also posted in Pakistan for a few months where he developed a sexual relationship with his maid, who it turned out was an ISI agent. A clerk in the embassy was summoned to Delhi, branded an ISI handle and arrested when the news leaked that the officer's maid was transferring sensitive data from her master's official residence in Islamabad to the headquarters of Pakistan's spying agency.

I had met this officer once and realised that his ultimate wish was to become governor of a state after retirement.

In any case, questioning a democracy at this stage is not a good idea particularly when the country has been growing economically at a faster pace than the neighbours.

We Indians feel good when comparing ourselves with Pakistan or Afghanistan or Nepal. We would have been like them had we not opened our doors to western trade and modernity at the cost of what many feared was economic slavery.

I don't know the future. But the present is better than the past. Only thing is that boredom is growing, and so are the number of perverts. Torture before rape is the latest fad among criminals. Playing games with the victim before killing them glorifies the criminal. Political parties notice them and race against each other to bring such perverts into their outfits.

FOURTEEN

● ● ● ● ● ● ● ●●●●●●●●●●●●●●●● ● ● ● ● ● ●

"**D**on't you think your daughter would have been alive if there had been proper laws in place?" I asked the father.

"Yes, if her friend, Kartik had shown some courage," he clicked his tongue, stood up, took a few steps towards a British woman correspondent from a news agency, took a couple of steps back, turned to me and said: "Look, I am a patriot. I love my country. I can make out you don't love your country. We must stop cursing a popular government. It would be an insult to the sacrifice of my daughter. I know that you do not like my words. But I don't care about you and people like you. The Prime Minister and Chief Ministers of many states are sad over the incident and eager to talk to me, help me."

Scolding me for 'cursing a popular government' and 'love for the country' were two different political propositions of the time. Badreshwar was, or not, a perfect conglomeration of the two opposing trends.

"People like you should live in Pakistan."

He looked at me in anger through his frog-like eyes and then walked towards the woman correspondent. Suddenly his mobile phone rang and he ran to a corner where he could be alone.

There was a glow in his eyes when he came back after talking for a minute on the phone. His voice quivered, not in fear but excitement. He looked at Someshwar and said, "It was Sri Ravi Maharaj. He has invited me to the south to meet him and discuss the problems in our society."

I knew Ravi Maharaj. He was a spiritual master. I had met him once in Allahabad, at the Mahakumbh along the confluence of the Ganga, the Yamuna and the mythical Saraswati.

There were over 150 people with Maharaj, including the wife of the owner of the newspaper I was working with at that time. This newspaper was popular in north India and had over 24 editions in the country.

They had booked 20 Swiss cottages in Mahakumbh. My colleagues and I were on duty to look after the cottage of Maharaj. The newspaper owner's wife had emphasised the need to ensure that there was to be a particular brand of mineral water in the toilet meant for Maharaj, as he wouldn't wash his backside with the water normally supplied by the local municipal administration or just any mineral water. He would wash and bathe only with the bottled water transported for him by a company directly from the Himalayas.

He also did not eat vegetables grown on Indian soil. The vegetables he consumed came from Britain and were calorie-less or less calorie. The rice and wheat he consumed were grown in the fields around his ashrams across the country. These items were brought to him in huge trucks.

Always wrapped in a shawl, Maharaj's likeness to Master Oogway from the movie *Kung Fu Panda* was striking. Especially so when he was in conversation with his devotees about the past, future and present.

One evening, while Maharaj was lecturing the wife of a divisional commissioner, her son sitting by her side, suddenly stood up and declared that the guru was repeating Oogway's dialogue. The mother slapped him and ordered him to sit. The boy obeyed. The guru smiled, as was his wont, but I could see he was not able to speak with the flow for which he was known.

Maharaj's favourite pastime in Mahakumbh was to give interviews to newspapers and television channels in a studio developed in his sprawling cottage.

Maharaj and his rich disciples enjoyed boating on the Ganga on the third day of Mahakumbh. While all of them touched the holy water, Maharaj didn't do that in fear of contracting a skin infection. On returning from the confluence, Maharaj went inside his tent for *prasad*. It is lunch or dinner for the common man and *prasad* for a 'holy soul'.

Then he sat in a corner and asked his expensively dressed disciples who had accompanied him from Delhi to receive his leftover food. "*Kripaya prasad graham karen* (Please accept the *prasad*)", the guru said in his usual soft voice. I saw my newspaper owner's wife fighting with the wife of an industrialist for it.

Maharaj jumped from his chair and began dancing. Then, he performed a magic trick and cashews appeared in his right hand. He went to the newspaper owner's wife, pulled her blouse and put the cashews into her cleavage. She was overwhelmed. She bowed and touched Maharaj's feet with her forehead.

"Love your country and eat cashew," the guru said, giving her the mantra of great living and moved towards the wife of the industrialist. He moved his left hand in the air similar to a heron moving its neck to catch its prey. Grapes appeared in his hand. He plucked one and put it in her mouth. She fell on his feet to kiss it.

I was surprised. I was unable to understand why I was not angry with the father of the rape victim. This silence was not my natural action. Perhaps I didn't want to hurt him. Or, maybe, I did not wish to be the centre of attraction in the village, where a large number of journalists from across the world had gathered. Many cameras were on and they would turn towards me. I was there to collect news not make news.

The recently acquired arrogance of the rape victim's father was the result of a complex decadent political system. I was trying to cook up reasons to remain calm.

I have heard that a certain international chain of fashion showrooms play music at a particular wavelength and maintain a specific temperature in different seasons. That helps them increase their business. The customers feel good for the first 20 minutes and then begin to get irritated. The idea is to ensure that the customer makes a purchase in the next 10 minutes, whatever he or she has selected in the first 20 minutes and leave so that the showroom can accommodate new customers every half an hour.

'Maybe he is right; I am wrong. Maybe I should be in Pakistan. Maybe I shouldn't question the Indian system. Maybe I am essentially an anti-national or the odd-one-out and my education was trash.'

Badreshwar was the face of the 21st Century. His ideological pattern had changed overnight. No university could inculcate this potential in anybody other than the political class.

I always advise people to stay away from this class as it could spoil and corrupt even the most innocent man on the earth.

The prime minister, chief ministers, politicians, bureaucrats, tax thieves and gurus cannot understand that life is present and the future is suffering. The father perhaps understood the pain of life till a few days ago. But he was upgraded quickly; his nerves transmitted the feelings to the brain to prevent him from cutting off or blocking the material edge. Was he lured into an illusion or surrealism? Or maybe he had plunged into a new world order.

I felt I was smiling all the time when the father was scolding me for not loving my country. This was his conclusion and much to my chagrin, I didn't question him.

Badreshwar was more interested in foreign journalists, particularly women, and that didn't surprise me.

The hangover of a majority of Indians for white-skinned people is no secret. And then a white woman! In college, we would stop talking and stare at foreigners when we saw them on campus. And don't ask what our reaction was when we saw a white woman.

The British know our extraordinary interest in our earlier rulers. They have no problem with us looking at them without blinking. But, they do have a problem if we look at their prince or princess.

A common man is a common man. We are hungover with the Raj. They have it for their rulers.

Their prince and princess were in India last year. I was assigned to cover their visit to the historical monuments. While I was busy jotting points in my notepad during one such visit, I noticed three British reporters carrying a reporter from a Hindi newspaper and tossing him towards the rear gate of the heritage building seconds after the prince and princess emerged from the front gate.

They shouted, "How dare you stare at our royal couple like that?"

The reporter fell on me. I fractured my middle finger while saving him from falling on the white marbled floor.

I am sure the British journalists would ask more uncomfortable questions to the father of a rape victim than I did. But he wouldn't behave badly to them. Instead, I saw him offering a white-skinned woman correspondent tea and snacks and answering her questions with a readily worn smile and politeness that I had earlier seen in Maharaj.

At the end of the interview with the British woman journalist, I overheard the father saying, "I want to visit the palace of your queen and also meet the prince to narrate to him my glorious daughter's life."

I didn't know why he was keen to be with the prince. Or, was it just an exercise to make the British woman happy? Or, had India suddenly become too small for him and he was thinking of expanding himself in the United Kingdom or even win?

FIFTEEN

•••••••••••••••••••••••••

I owe myself an explanation as to why I was getting so involved in this story without being able to collect any relevant information.

It would be painful for any human being to assimilate the fact that a girl, who had dreamt of a great future, had been physically crushed forever by some rapists. The way they committed the crime was an indication that they were trained for the job. Or, maybe they had committed similar crimes so frequently and got away with it that they had done this to their latest prey with the skills of a professional.

But I was never so tense before. I was not so tense even when my best friend was crushed under an army officer's car with similar skill. Kancha Singh loved roaming across India on his motorcycle and had gone to a Himalayan state on one such venture. He had parked his motorcycle by the side of the road and was talking to his friend on his mobile phone. A car came towards him in reverse gear at full speed and killed him. An army officer was in the driver's seat.

There had been an army deployment in that place for decades, and in government parlance, it was known as a 'disturbed area'. This gave them the allowance to unleash all possible terror against their people.

There were allegations of mass killing, rape and illegal detention against a force or a government, forgetting that bringing peace to this place is the primary job.

It may be that 75 per cent of them don't forget their jobs. But 25 per cent don't remember that they are not made to terrorise and physically assault fellow citizens.

What will these 25 per cent do if they don't find anybody to terrorise or kill? I have heard that they are 1,50,000 out of a total of 6,00,000 in the Himalayan state. What will they do if they are sent back to their camps in Pune, Lucknow or Patna?

Two weeks after the 'accidental death', I read the statement of an officer in the Ministry of Defence. He said my friend was a Pakistani agent and roaming in the cantonment area to collect sensitive information about the army. As per the officer, a terrorist group had imparted training to Kancha in Pakistan.

I lived in Allahabad for seven years and we would meet each other almost every alternate day. I did not see any aberration in my friend.

The personnel from the Ministry of Defence also said that my friend was killed in a gun battle. But my friend had called his father minutes after the accident and told him everything before he succumbed to the injuries.

Nationalist India had confirmed that my friend was a hardcore terrorist involved in many blast cases across the country. It was a mystery only for a handful of people whether he died under the wheels of an army officer's car or killed by an army bullet. Or, if he was injured and later shot dead. But it was clear to me and his other friends that whatever happened to him, was the work of highly skilled people, who knew to kill and cover-up.

I once faced a similar situation in Allahabad. An air force officer driving a Maruti Gypsy hit me while I was passing through Bamrauli Air Force area on my scooter. He ignored the red light and cut the road as if chasing me. I was a stranger to him. The next day, I went to the Public Relation Officer of the force and told him about the incident. He laughed it off and told me that the officer was recently transferred from a battle zone to Allahabad and didn't know peacetime rules.

SIXTEEN

●●●●●●●●●●⋯⋯⋯●●●●●●●●●

I decided to meet the victim's boyfriend. He had also returned to Varanasi, his hometown, some 70 km from his girlfriend's village.

My photographer had heard me interviewing the father and listened to his patriotic sermon. But he didn't ask me about it.

We went to a *dhaba* on our way to Varanasi, finished our ablutions, brushed our teeth and drank tea. I was in a hurry to meet Kartik. We bought apples and bananas and ate them in the car to save time.

We reached the boyfriend's palatial house at around 2:00 PM. Many media persons were already there. A servant came out, took my visiting card and returned.

He came out after half an hour and declared, "There are nine media persons before you. You have to wait."

I nodded. Although we wanted to go to a nice restaurant and eat good food, I didn't want to miss the chance to meet and interview the boyfriend.

The driver was either sleeping in his seat or listening to Bhojpuri songs. In one of the songs, the male voice would ask the women when she would lift her *ghaghra*. The female voice replies that she would when her parents leave the house to go to a religious fair in the village. In another song, the woman invites her lover to her house in the afternoon when her father would be in the field and her mother with the neighbours.

Nahid had made friends among the television reporters. He was discussing something with them, his right hand in the shape of a bowl and moving it as if placing a lid on it.

My turn came at 10:00 PM. The servant came and took me in.

It was a big hall without a window, just an old green carpet on the floor and two doors with stripped, synthetic curtains. It had not been washed in the recent past. There was a dining table and four chairs in a corner. There were photos in frames hanging on the walls. In some, state politicians in saffron stood or sat with a middle-aged man. I presumed he must be the father of the boyfriend.

We sat on a long black sofa from which a foul smell emanated.

The boyfriend came in after 10 minutes and stood in the middle of the hall, expecting us to walk towards him.

He stood with his legs slightly apart, his hands in the pockets of his jeans and his eyes fixed on the ground.

We stood and took a few steps towards him. He was not looking at us.

"How are you?" I started the conversation.

Kartik remained silent for about two minutes and then abruptly askcd: "How much?"

I was baffled.

"How much what? I don't understand you."

"How much will you pay for this interview?"

I never dreamt of facing such a question in my career. However, I recently heard from a journalist friend that a Hindi woman writer who had become a celebrity after writing a novel on the plight of a woman asked reporters to pay her for the interviews.

She was not a big writer until a few months ago. The feeling of greatness had entered her soon after the success of her book. It is an ailment from which many Hindi and English writers suffer.

I knew an Indian English writer who was a teacher at a college in London. He would secretly give cash to the reporters and ask them to pay him half the amount in the presence of other reporters to prove that he was being paid for his interviews. I once met him in a small restaurant in Bangalore. In the one hour I conversed with him, he boasted continuously of his popularity.

"I couldn't leave my chair in Delhi for 14 hours after arriving from London because one or another reporter was eager to interview me. Many television channels were willing to pay me in pounds for a 30-minute interview," he said as if he was obliging me with a free-of-cost interview. He bore a striking similarity to Badreshwar.

I pretended that I was listening to the writer with appreciation. But I decided not to file the interview, ever.

"I am sorry, we don't pay an interviewee," I replied to Kartik.

"Then I cannot give you an interview," he said. Kartik was straightforward but rough.

SEVENTEEN

• • • • • • • • • ••••••••••••••• • • • • • •

Something about Kartik was making me uncomfortable and restless. I was sure I had met him before.

"Do I know you?" I asked him.

He looked directly into my eyes.

"You were there in a bar in Paharganj a few days before the incident. You were carrying a revolver and told me you could fix anybody if I needed," I reminded him.

There was an uneasy calm between us for about 40 seconds.

When I had seen him in Paharganj, his face seemed dehydrated. Today, his eyes were glazed.

A fellow student, who used to eat lunch with me in a cheap restaurant in Allahabad's Alenganj, would joke that there was a strong reason behind the victory of a hero in the Hindi cinema over the villains.

"The hero looks weaker than the villain but he beats the villain easily because he eats meals cooked by his mother. If you notice, the villain always eats in a restaurant."

The boyfriend must be eating food cooked by his mother these days and so he was looking better than before.

Kartik broke the silence, "Aah. Maybe. I was drunk that day."

"I also saw you with a middle-aged woman entering a hotel." I was gaping at him.

"I was frustrated that evening. Anyway, I am leaving for Delhi now because I have to be on television. Do you know how much they are paying me for a 30-minute interview?" He told me the name of the news channel.

I didn't feel like asking him how much. But he wanted me to know.

"Rs 10 lakhs." There was pride in his voice, the kind of pride I had felt in the voice of Badreshwar when he was talking about his patriotism.

I knew that the owner of the news channel, that had invited the boyfriend, had started his career only 10 years ago with contracts to cap government-owned paddy kept in open fields in Chhattisgarh and Madhya Pradesh with plastic sheets. He started his business with Rs 10 crore and presently he had an empire with Rs 10,000 crore turnover. He was the owner of six news and entertainment channels.

The boyfriend stalked back and forth and then left the hall without waiting for my reaction.

We ran to the cab, as I wanted to get to a decent hotel, shower, eat good food and sleep on a proper bed. I thought it would be better to think about the story in the morning.

As I was about to get into the car, I saw the servant coming towards me. Kartik's father wanted to meet me.

We entered the hall again. A man in his late 50s welcomed us and asked the servant to bring tea.

I was right. It was the same person in the photos with the politicians.

He asked Nahid to wait outside and then said, "I respect journalists and want to make a request."

"My son is a dolt. He is young and enjoys life without taking basic care of anything... I have suffered a lot in my life. Today I have everything because of my hard work... My father was a freedom fighter. We belong to a patriotic family. But the new generation has no respect for hard work. They are born to enjoy life. It is natural... But my son is also a nationalist like me. You can see he has placed a national flag on the dashboard of his car. I request you to understand this and not write about your meeting with him in the Delhi bar. I will pay you Rs 2 lakh to keep this secret."

Nobody had ever offered me a bribe barring the upcoming politician who wanted to pay for diesel out of sympathy.

I shivered in my warm clothes.

"No. It's okay," I replied.

The reporter in me was still alert.

"The father of the girl was saying your son could have saved her by showing a little courage when the rapists pounced on her," I said.

"I heard this on a news channel. Tell him to shut his mouth. Or my son, the sole witness of the incident, will refuse to identify the rapists," came his reply.

"I am aware that you know the law very well."

"I also know people who play with the law," he was smiling.

I stood up.

"Please wait," he requested, then added, "There are editors on the payroll of many of my friends. Either you accept my offer or I will meet your editor. Don't think he will be an exception."

I rushed out to the car without looking back. I needed a luxurious bath and a refreshing meal.

Nahid was waiting for me. He realised that I was disturbed. He didn't ask me anything.

That's the best thing about him. He knows when to remain silent.

I was thinking about the ignorant arrogance of Badreshwar and the recklessness of the boyfriend and his father. Whatever was in them was a bold signature of the same complex decadent political system I have often mentioned in my conversations with friends in recent months.

However, I was not able to make out whether I was witnessing two isolated cases or if they were closely connected.

Am I outdated? Did their ideological pattern suggest they were true citizens of 21st Century India?

She loved him and this was the only reason he was her boyfriend. She loved him; he assaulted her emotionally, psychologically and perhaps physically before she met her killers in the cab. She loved a social criminal; some hardcore criminals killed her.

You can identify a hardcore criminal but what about a social criminal?

I had many questions. And I knew that I knew the answers. But that was not enough to save a dreamer from getting killed in the course of looking for a better future than her present.

EIGHTEEN

●●●●●●●●●●●●●●············●●●●●●●●●●●●●

I was in Varanasi and I loved this city because of its religious hegemony, corrupted art and intense sexually laden invectives that are constantly overheard in its narrow streets. Developed around Kashi, an ancient town, the city is sitting on a cultural bomb. There are musicians, Hindi writers and ruffians who have the potential to revolutionise art and culture in their style.

However, the political system seems to have gradually corrupted them. My friend Chattopadhyay, who lives in this city, says that the corrupt writers and dishonest artists living here are such dogs that they will lick your heel if you put them on the ground and your cheeks when you lift them in your laps.

"They can efficiently sing a holy song or a religious couplet at the door of a honeymooning couple," he would say.

Once Chattopadhyay wrote four lines in Sanskrit and asked his classical singer friend to sing them at a concert they were attending.

The singer of a local *gharana* asked Chattopadhyay its meaning and my friend told him that it was in honour of the four most important Hindu pilgrimage centres.

The singer quickly rehearsed the lines and sang it amid thunderous applause. There were scholars of Sanskrit also in the audience. They understood the meaning of those four lines. The couplet was a detailed narration of every religion's lovemaking habits.

The Sanskrit scholars stood as soon as the singer finished and moved towards him. Chattopadhyay and his friends immediately intervened and made a passage for the singer to escape.

"He is a well-known singer. He is also close to a big politician. But I wanted to prove that he is a *chootiya* (stupid)," said Chattopadhyay, whose father was an employee of the Indian Railways and had settled in Varanasi. He told me this story while having *roti* and *dal* in a *dhaba* near Assi Ghat a few years ago.

The boyfriend I met today was a perfect resident of this ancient city.

NINETEEN

● ●

I had seen Kartik with a prostitute in Paharganj that evening. It is not that I have contempt for those who go for paid sex.

I have an extremely enterprising good friend who lives in Bombay. One day, he visited a brothel early in the afternoon and asked a prostitute what her rate was. She said Rs 2000 for 30 minutes.

"I have Rs 200 only."

"Get lost, you bastard."

He returned after two hours.

"How much?"

"Pay me Rs 1000."

"No. I have Rs 200 only."

"Try elsewhere."

He came back again after two hours.

"Are you ready for Rs 200?"

"No."

My friend went there for the last time at around 10 pm.

"You are a real bastard. Come and finish it in 15 minutes. Pay me Rs 200 in advance, you pig."

Samsher is a liberated man. It is not that he cannot pay Rs 2000 for 30 minutes. He wanted to test whether he still had his marketing skills. And at the same time, he wanted his fantasy to come true at a budget he had set for himself.

He has been my friend for a long time because he never discusses politics with me. While in university, he was a theatre artist and wanted to pursue a career in Bollywood. Presently, he is an assistant director with a famous filmmaker for a middlebrow movie. There was inconsistency in his earnings and his parents didn't like this. His father, a staunch Brahmin, was a clerk in the agriculture department and used to get paid on the first day of every month. He wanted his son to be in such a job. But my friend didn't think himself fit for it.

Initially, Samsher joined a newspaper as a circulation executive and eventually rose to the position of manager in three years before boarding a train to Bombay.

There was another friend of mine, who loved putting his head on the breasts of a prostitute. Born in a milkman's family, he had lots of money and used to pay her Rs 5000 for a night.

Later, he cracked the Indian Administrative Service and was posted as an officer in the national capital.

We knew if he was not in his hostel room, he would be with Sasha Darling, the prostitute.

We added Darling to Sasha's name. He had taken me to see her. She looked like a western model. We contemplated whether Sasha Darling was of an Indian and English lineage.

But Sasha Darling told her lover that she was from Dholpur in Rajasthan. Her parents had donated her to a village temple when she was six-year-old. The temple of the local goddess propagated prostitution as sacred work.

The grandfather of a local politician had founded the temple. The politician later became the family welfare minister of his state.

I lost touch with this milkman-turned-bureaucrat after he became an officer of the elite cadre.

I recently read in a newspaper that Brahmin policemen had attacked him when he was sitting in a bar with friends. The same news also said that earlier he was caught in a hotel room with the wife of a politician.

I don't have any contempt for these friends because it is their habit to do such things.

TWENTY

●●●●●●●●●●●●●●●●●●●●●●●●●●●●●●

Most of the rooms in the hotel were vacant. The receptionist was yawning continuously while checking me in. He appeared to be a lazy man except when woman employees passed by the reception. Then he looked up from the computer screen and stared at them, moving his eyeballs mysteriously till she looked back and smiled.

He tried to initiate a conversation with them, ignoring the customer waiting for the booking to be registered in the thick register, after entering the details in the computer.

At least four women passed by while I was waiting for my key. While all of them smiled back at him, only one of them talked to him.

"Stop looking like this, don't keep the guest waiting," the last of the four told him and turned to me: "Have a nice time, sir."

"Um...hm." I had not expected that she would still remember the courtesy of wishing a customer when her colleague was staring at her as if he would swallow her in one go.

He gave us a nice room. I could see a reddish fog through the window. There were droplets stuck to the lower portion of the windowpanes suggesting that it had begun drizzling.

Tired but restless, sleep was far from me. I tried to deceive myself, thinking that it was because of the photographer's snore from the next bed.

When in Delhi, Nahid does not drink liquor. But once out of the city, he loved drinking in the evening. Fridays or Ramadan don't make a difference to him outside the invisible magnetic boundary of his home, where he lives with his parents, wife and son.

Tonight, in 45 minutes he finished more than a quarter bottle and a plate of snacks by the time I sipped my 120 ml. I called for room service for dinner and ate it without bothering him.

My company doesn't reimburse the travel expense of a photographer. There is a plan in the pipeline to abolish the photography department. In that case, I would have to carry a camera and be designated reporter-cum-photographer. I am not sure if there would also be editor-cum-photographer or executive editor-cum-photographer or editor-in-chief-cum photographer.

Recently, a lady – daughter of a bureaucrat – joined the newspaper as vice-president, of the human resources department. On the very first day, she declared that reporters should carry cameras because she would soon be shutting the department to save money for the company.

I spontaneously crossed the hierarchical boundary and had a heated exchange of words with her a few days later. She said many newspapers in the world had done so. I asked her to give me the names of the newspapers.

She thought for a while, her big, beautiful eyes looking out of the window of her chamber on the fifth floor. Suddenly she declared: "The reporters in the west take photographs of Hollywood stars romancing on the beaches."

"They are paparazzi and the newspapers provide them helicopters and the costliest of equipment for such assignments." I tried to pin her down with the help of borrowed and unconfirmed knowledge.

She looked at me for a few seconds, her eyes burning with anger, looking extremely beautiful.

My editor was sitting beside me. But he didn't intervene. The meeting ended in 90 seconds. Later in the evening, the editor congratulated me and said, "I am happy that you dared to react."

I wanted to say: "I am unhappy because you were looking for a rat hole to hide your face." But I answered him with a smile.

TWENTY-ONE

●●●●●●●●●●●●●●●●●●●●●●●●●

Something was keeping me awake that night.

I do not have a sleeping disorder. This has never happened to me before. Never have I attached so much importance to a story or its characters. I have always, in my decade-old career, behaved professionally.

I have dedicated sources in the government and political parties who make my job easy. I also have people in authority who have given me a carte blanche to quote them to complete my copy even without talking to them. All I needed was to know the line they would take on such and such issue.

Tonight I realised that I wouldn't be able to write the follow-up stories on this gang-rape case if I didn't seriously detach myself from the subjects. I knew that I was going to lose the opportunity to report on something, which would be remembered for many decades in India and abroad. Like other reporters, I also live in hope that my stories will change the world, force a Prime Minister to step down or pull down a government.

I heard about a surgeon, who had done thousands of operations of a certain kind but failed when his mother was on the operation table. She died and thereafter he never performed any more operations.

He retired to Haridwar, a Hindu religious town, and ran an Ayurveda clinic with the help of doctors of the discipline.

Now I realise why good doctors don't interact with their patients much.

It normally takes me one hour to collect information and 20 minutes to file a story. However, I have been roaming for the last two days for this rape and murder case and don't feel like writing even a word.

My editor called me last evening when I was waiting to meet the boyfriend and asked for a 700-word copy. I told him without any hesitation that I was disillusioned with everything that I heard or saw in the course of following the story. He thought I was unwell and said, "I can send a reporter from here to complete the job if you are not feeling well. You can come back. Don't feel bad. It happens. You have been doing a great job in past. Heaven will not fall if you don't do one story."

"Please use agency copies for daily developments. I want to be here," I replied, offended.

"I'll file my stories when I get back to Delhi."

"It may become irrelevant by that time," he said.

The editor quickly rephrased his words: "Ok, ok. No problem. Please go ahead with your plan. I'll ask someone in Delhi to follow the daily stories on the subject from here."

TWENTY-TWO

●●●●●●●●●●●●⋯⋯⋯⋯⋯●●●●●●●●●●

My editor is a good soul if I ignored his spinelessness. He would try to understand me even though he wouldn't be able to reach my mind.

As I said before, his only problem was that he bowed before the management on any and every issue. He could even beg for an advertisement or sponsorship for a conclave of the newspaper from a politician or an industrialist.

"We should bring the company to breakeven." This was his favourite dialogue. Many of us shudder when we hear this as 'breakeven' means sacrificing editorial staff.

One day, our proprietor was invited by a club to lecture on editorial content. I accompanied the editor to the venue of the lecture.

The proprietor, a religious person, delivered his speech with great energy.

"Earlier, we used to appoint strong editors. Later, I realised that a strong editor is expensive. He will demand a high salary and will also appoint reporters and sub-editors on high salaries. Now we appoint only 'neuter' editors. They are good for the health of the newspaper."

On our way back, I asked the editor for the meaning of 'neuter'.

"I don't know," he replied.

"Let me check in the online dictionary," I said.

"Leave it," he said, looking out of the window. It was a melancholy look.

I didn't look for the meaning at that time.

Later, I found it meant 'eunuch'.

I wondered how the proprietor could make out that such and such a person would be a 'neuter' editor. I asked one of my friends during a drinking session in Paharganj. Amid guffaws, he said, "Maybe he pulls down the pants of the interviewees before taking a decision."

But this editor was better than many of my previous editors. Or at least I found him to be better than others.

TWENTY-THREE

●●●●●●●●●●●●⋯⋯⋯⋯⋯●●●●●●●●●●

My first job was with a weekly newspaper in Uttar Pradesh. The editor was an American lady. She was a nice human being. But she didn't understand the difference between the monkey god – Bajrang Bali and a Hindu organisation, which was allegedly involved in violence and murder in several parts of the country.

One day, she sacked a district reporter alleging that he didn't follow her instruction on how to file a story on a congregation of the organisation going on in the old city area of Allahabad. The reporter kept telling her that it was not the organisation but a ritual organised by a Hindu family to appease the monkey god.

She avoided making decisions without consulting the management. The management would deduct a week's salary if our story didn't get published in an edition.

The owner of the newspaper was also a lady. She was in love with her manager. I once caught them making love between the stacks of newspapers in the manager's room. I entered his room to demand a Rs 1000 advance.

They remained still for a few seconds. The manager then stretched his neck above the stacks of newspapers and asked me the reason behind my unwarranted entry into the room. I reminded him about my application for an advance.

"Take the money from the pocket of my pant on the table and get lost," he said in an extraordinarily soft voice.

I saw her smiling; giving me a reason to believe that she didn't dislike me looking at them cuddling.

A few months later, the manager ran away with several lakhs of cash. The owner couldn't handle the setback. She lost her mental balance and the newspaper closed.

Thereafter, I joined a soft-porn magazine. There, I looked after its four literary pages. We partied every evening in the office. There were also occasions when I couldn't get back home and slept on the sofa in the visitor's room of the office.

I heard girls and women approached the owner-cum-editor for nude photoshoots. He paid them handsomely for the pictures. One day, following a complaint from a bureaucrat, there was a police raid and the magazine closed down. That week's edition carried a front-page nude picture of the officer's daughter. We heard that the owner-cum-editor, a chain smoker and an alcoholic, had promised her a break in a Bollywood movie in return for pictures of her naked in a stable.

The father of the owner-cum-editor published pulp fiction in his press in the past. There were writers at that time who could write a 400-page novel in one night. All they needed was Rs 1000 to buy a bottle of alcohol and dinner at a roadside *dhaba*. They would write the novel there, sitting on a bamboo and rope cot. They were popular among the regular long-distance railway passengers. Ramu, a tall, dark man was one such novelist, who couldn't write even a line without being drunk.

Many writers in those days were inspired by Irwin Allen Ginsberg. I heard from some cheap Hindi authors of Allahabad and Calcutta that he inspired aspiring writers to visit a prostitute in a brothel and then begin a novel or even a poem. Many followed his advice meticulously. As a result, many of them died of syphilis. AIDS may have been the cause of some deaths, but they may not have known as the disease was yet unknown to the scientists of that time.

Ginsberg's influence was such that many middle-aged people who survived despite their lifestyle believed that the American writer was doing a holy job, destroying a generation. They believed, they were his successors, assigned to destroy the next generation of promising writers.

When the son of the pulp publisher took over from his father, he decided to modernise everything from the press to the content of the publication. He planned and we realised his dream of bringing out a magazine similar to *Playboy*.

He was also into the construction business.

Within a month of joining, I was in charge of the literary section of the magazine because most of the people left for one reason or another. The managing editor, who was working simultaneously with a daily newspaper, never came to the office. At least I never saw him there. He would give directions over the phone.

The police raided the office and most of the staff went underground. They surfaced after 60 days when cases against them were withdrawn because of lack of evidence.

I was taken to the police station and detained for four hours. There was nothing against me because I showed them my appointment letter as a literary editor.

The owner-cum-editor was arrested and jailed for a few days. He re-launched the magazine with a new team after he was released from jail.

By then, I had joined a daily newspaper where my previous managing editor was working. My job in this newspaper was to look after a feature page.

My editor was a homosexual.

Page making was done manually. There was a paste-up artist who warned me on the first day.

"At any cost, don't go to the darkroom with the editor," he said in a serious and mysterious voice while cutting and arranging each column of a page set on a wooden board.

The editor was in the habit of shaking hands often, for no reason. Every time he shook my hand he would rub his index finger on my palm. I told the paste-up artist about this. He laughed heartily and said, "It is a suggestion. He has set his eyes on you. He is trying to tell you about his intentions."

One day, when I went to show an edited copy to him, he took my left hand in his hands and started caressing it. I didn't feel comfortable and tried to pull my hand away from him. But he had held it tight. I don't know what happened to me but I slapped him with my right hand.

He released my hand immediately and I came out of his chamber. The next day, he shifted me to the general desk and reduced my salary by 30 per cent.

"Mr Ramayan Prasad is not able to handle the feature page efficiently." A notice signed by him was plastered on the notice board.

I decided to fight back. I went to the guesthouse where the owner of the newspaper was staying for the past few days.

I walked through the garden of the guesthouse and entered an open door. There I found Mr Dubey, the owner of the newspaper, undressing a teenage girl. Another girl of almost the same age was standing beside her, giggling. She was naked.

I had seen the two girls before in the office. They were a stringer's sisters. The stringer moonlighted as a lawyer.

I went off and never tried to meet the owner again. Two weeks later, the stringer was promoted to the post of assistant editor.

Thereafter, I moved to Delhi. Initially, I was with a group where most of my assignments were to appease the leaders of a particular political party. The proprietor would happily convert his magazines into a pamphlet of that political party. He also owned one of the biggest printing presses in the country.

He was also the editor. A leader of a political party, during an election campaign in Uttar Pradesh, threw him off the stage.

As if this insult was not enough for him, a few days later he entered the chamber of the president of the party. But the security personnel of the party chief shoved him out when he refused to leave. All the while he kept stressing that he was 'editor of the most successful publication in India'.

Still, he deployed four reporters including me to write in praise of those leaders. Their pictures repeatedly appeared on the cover pages of the magazine and the owner would personally meet the leaders to present a copy. One day, he declared in the morning meeting that at least two big leaders of that party had offered him tea, which he politely refused because he wanted to set an example of honesty and integrity before his staff.

TWENTY-FOUR

●●●●●●●●●···············●●●●●●●●●

I woke up at around 12:30 pm. My photographer visited Lanka Market, where we were staying and bought me a book.

He was amused to see me awake.

"What had happened to you last night?"

"What?"

"You were asking me repeatedly whether I have ever loved a woman who was raped and killed."

"You also wanted to know how we could keep alive a woman who had been killed?'

I went to the washroom without replying. I shaved and took a shower. Nahid prepared tea for me with the electric kettle in the room and then suggested I read a few pages of the book he had bought for me.

The name of the book was *Evolution*. It was printed in 1933 by S. Amar Singh at Model Electric Press, Lahore and published by Khan Sahib Agha Mohammad Sultan Mirza, Rawalpindi.

"Not that they conquered India; India forced them to assume sovereignty over her. This was the highest act of patriotism that our forefathers could do, looking to the state of anarchy and confusion that was eating away the life of the country. If left alone, India would have either

cut herself asunder or would have been a satrapy of the Napoleonic Empire," it read.

Patriotism is unpredictable. I felt this in 1998 when five nuclear tests were done in a series. I was having lunch in a restaurant in the Alenganj area of Allahabad. That was my usual place for the past many months. Many students at the University of Allahabad were regular customers there.

The owner of the restaurant, a heavy, dark man who always remained bare above his waist, was talking about "the establishment of Hindu pride" through the nuclear test. The majority of students were also talking about it excitedly and dubbing it as a patriotic step by the government.

I said spontaneously, "Such firecrackers don't make any sense in a world where every country, even Pakistan, is nuclear rich."

Suddenly, I realised that there was pin-drop silence in the restaurant and everyone was looking at me.

The students sitting beside me finished their lunch unusually fast and left.

The restaurant owner, who was making *chapatis*, came to me and said, "Do not go out for some time. I am looking for someone who can help you get away without getting hurt.'

He came to me again after a few minutes and said, "There is a bicycle at the gate. Some students are angry with you and have gone to bring their friends to beat you up. Take the bicycle and run away from here. And please don't come to my restaurant for at least a week."

I had heard about a particular kind of patriotism from the leader of an organisation in 1990. His name was Acharya Govind.

"Not posing questions to those whom you trust is real patriotism. You must not think for a second if I ask you to jump in a well," he was addressing a gathering of like-minded people.

"We are a kind of hardcore patriots. This is why we survive amid many odds. Our organisations were banned many times. But we have hundreds of legs – just like centipedes. You impose a ban against one leg and the other leg gets activated. The centipede can move easily even if some of its legs are damaged. Nobody can stop us from pursuing patriotism. The centipede can reach its destination even if many of its legs are removed. Nobody can stop the centipede. Similarly, nobody can stop us."

After the meeting, I requested one of my acquaintances to introduce me to Acharya Govind. He took me to a small room in a corner of the ground where the meeting was held.

"Where do you come from?" Govind asked me.

"Bihar."

"Where in Bihar?"

"Darbhanga."

"Where in Darbhanga?"

"Jale."

"Jale?"

"Yes."

"It is a Muslim village," he said.

"Yes, I know that," I answered.

There is a big vegetable and mutton market in Jale. I used to visit the market with my father when I was studying in a village school. We bought mutton there.

There was also a temple in the outskirts of the village, which we visited during Navratri puja.

There was nothing unusual about the village. At least I never noticed anything unusual.

"How do you know about this village?"

"I know every village that shouldn't exist on earth," he said bluntly.

"I have a happy memory of this village. They are peace-loving people." I protested and then added after a gap of a few seconds: "A centipede can be stopped even if its head is crushed."

He picked up an iron chain from an open shelf near his chair. It was thinner than a dog chain and longer than the one used as a key chain by fashionable rural youths, who ride motorcycles.

Govind was moving it around his index finger clockwise and anti-clockwise.

I decided to leave.

"Keep meeting me," he said.

Every word of patriotism and the moving chain in his hand came to my mind.

I got out of the restaurant, picked up the cycle and escaped.

TWENTY-FIVE

•••••••••••••••••••••••••••

*E*volution started haunting me. I saw from the corner of my left eye that Nahid was watching for my reaction or a change in my facial expression.

I flipped through the pages of the book and noticed he had underlined one more paragraph.

"The greatest act of patriotism is to support and cooperate with the present regime in working out the destiny of India."

He took the book from me, opened a page and read aloud:

"Thinkers and philosophers have openly declared that you'll never have a quiet world till you knock patriotism out of the human race."

We both laughed heartily and then went to the restaurant downstairs.

We had lunch and decided to visit the victim's village in Bhadohi again.

TWENTY-SIX

●●●●●●●●●●●●●●●●●●●●●●

Badreshwar was sitting on the same jute cot as yesterday. He was receiving and making phone calls and talking to reporters in between.

He had given me a dressing-down earlier while sitting on this same cot.

I could make out from the body language that he was talking to someone very important on the phone.

After every such call, he would move his face left and right like a duck, perhaps trying to make eye contact with his relatives and fellow villagers who were hanging around to see how media posed a question and how extraordinarily well he answered it.

There were still many reporters camping there. My turn came after two hours.

The curious villagers did not want to go home for breakfast, lunch or dinner. A youth, with his hand on the shoulder of another, was hungrily staring at an English woman journalist and singing in Bhojpuri in a low voice: "Centre *se* centre *milao re, hamra baap ke patohiya* (My father's daughter-in-law, let your centre meet mine)."

"Do you feel comfortable with the queries of these English journalists?" I tried to initiate the conversation with him again.

I was prepared for any kind of humiliating reaction from him. I had committed to myself that I would never respond in the same manner.

"I can survive because of them. They reported the revolution which took place in the country following the incident," he said in a firm voice, taking a long pause after every sentence.

"You cannot imagine the struggles in my life. I work eight hours a day plus eight more hours of overtime. It takes two hours to reach the workplace from my home in Delhi. I have never slept more than three hours a night. I have suffered unparalleled pain in my life. And now you can see what happened to my daughter. The gods must be testing my patience. But He has ultimately recognised my struggle and revolutionised India. I want an Ashoka Chakra for my daughter posthumously."

I quickly googled Neerja Bhanot on my mobile phone to tell him why India's highest peacetime award was conferred on her, a flight attendant with Pan Am Flight 73.

"She died saving passengers from the Libyan backed Palestinian Abu Nidal group who had hijacked a flight on September 5, 1986. While three members in the cockpit managed to flee from the aircraft at Karachi airport, she, the senior-most cabin crew, remained. Since the terrorists wanted to kill all American passengers, she and her colleague managed to hide the passports of 41 Americans. Later, when the terrorists opened fire to kill the passengers, she opened the emergency door to help them escape. She was killed in the shooting while protecting three children." I read aloud from a website and then translated it into Hindi for him.

"You fail to understand that *Anot*-Bhanot didn't bring revolution in the country. My daughter did," Badreshwar stressed.

"Can I meet your wife?" I asked him.

He denied the request instantly.

"The women in my family live in *ghunghat* and don't go out of the house without being accompanied by their father, husband or sons. They cannot interact with strangers. Even my mother, who is 80 years old, will not like talking to a stranger. We belong to the best caste among the upper castes. My name is Badreshwar Singh and I am a Thakur."

I knew he was not a Thakur. He told the foreign reporters his surname was Singh.

I returned to Varanasi the same evening and Delhi the next day.

TWENTY-SEVEN

•••••••••••·············•••••••••••

Since there was someone else covering the day-to-day stories from Delhi, I decided a week later to take leave and meet Badreshwar, who had returned from Bhadohi. His neighbours in the semi-slum on the outskirts of Laxmi Nagar told me that they had shifted to a two-bedroom apartment in the Patparganj area, which was given to them by the government.

Their single-room house was locked and a five or six-year-old girl was standing outside its door with a doll in her hand.

"What are you doing here?" I asked.

"I am waiting for *didi*. She keeps this doll on her lap whenever she teaches us. But her brother threw it out and left. I am waiting for *didi* to return this to her and ask her when she will teach me."

It was drizzling.

I took the address from a neighbour and reached their new house.

There were two constables at the door. The father responded to the knock and opened the door.

Badreshwar's face was expressionless. But he moved aside allowing me to enter his house. I sat there on a new sofa; remained silent for about one minute and then apologised for bothering him again.

"Where do you see the revolution now? The one you spoke to me about in the village? Are you satisfied with whatever happened after the unfortunate incident? Do you see any major change in the country?"

"I am sure media and NGOs will keep the fire alive. She was not only my daughter...she was the daughter of India...daughter of the world." I stood up before he could finish.

"Sorry, I forgot I had an assignment to complete by this afternoon. I'll be back soon."

As I came out of the lift of the apartment, I saw a serious-looking man, accompanied by four policemen and two assistants carrying thick files waiting for the lift. A constable asked me the number of Badreshwar's flat.

"Fourth floor, just in front of the lift," I answered and left.

TWENTY-EIGHT

●●●●●●●●●·················●●●●●●●

Sitting idly in my flat a month later, I read a scroll on a news channel that the institute where the victim was a student had announced that they would sponsor the education of five poor students and the scheme would be named after Roshni.

I couldn't resist calling Badreshwar on the mobile number he had given me during one of our meetings.

His eldest son, Aniket, who was doing his intermediate, answered.

"We have read in the newspaper about the announcement of the institute. I don't know why the principal of the college changed his mind. He told us that he wanted to return the fees which my sister had paid for two years," he said.

I could hear the sound of fast, loud Hindi music in the background.

"Are you enjoying the music?"

"Oh, not exactly," Aniket replied, "I am having lunch in a restaurant in Connaught Place with my friends. Please call me later if you want to ask me more questions."

I told him I wanted to talk to his father.

"He is very busy these days. He and my mom are working for an NGO and have hardly any time," he replied energetically and disconnected.

TWENTY-NINE

●●●●●●●●●●⋯⋯⋯⋯⋯●●●●●●●●●

I was restless. I was trying to convince myself that I shouldn't be so sensitive about the happenings around me or else I would lose my mental balance and interest in life. However, there was hardly a night after my return from Bhadohi and Varanasi that I didn't dream about the rape and murder of a girl. While there would be different criminals, the face of the victim remained the same every time, maybe her age changed at times.

I called Aniket again after a few days.

"How is life, boss? Did you dispose of your house in Laxmi Nagar? Do you ever meet your former neighbours?" I asked him as soon as he picked up the phone.

"Our neighbours are people with a lower class mentality. They don't think about development, patriotism and about the positive things in life. So we don't meet them now," he said.

"I wanted to talk to your father also. Can you please give him the phone?"

"No, papa is busy at the moment. He is also not interested in talking to reporters. But we are thinking of joining a protest movement organised by the students of Jawaharlal Nehru University next week.

He wants to tell the students how they should launch a successful movement," Aniket replied.

Although I didn't write anything, this news appeared in a few papers the next morning.

THIRTY

●●●●●●●●●●●●●●●●●●●●●●●●●

Three days after my last conversation with Aniket, I read in the newspapers that some ministers visited the family and promised them more benefits.

I called the brother again and asked what the ministers said.

"The ministers were here to enquire about my education. They were concerned about our future. I told them that I am unable to concentrate on my studies after the horrible incident involving my sister. They promised me a job soon," he said.

"When are the university students planning to hold the protest?"

"They have shelved the idea because my father is not willing to join them."

Although it was none of my business, I asked him how he performed in school.

I could make out that he didn't like the question.

"How does that matter to you?" he asked.

"I am trying to understand what kind of job would suit you. What exactly the government can do for you?"

"I got 45 per cent in matriculation and 47 per cent in the first year of intermediate. But I can improve in future."

I again asked him to give the phone to his father. This time I was lucky.

"So what kinds of changes have come into your life?" I asked the father.

"As you know we have shifted to a two-bedroom flat but it would be better if the government gives us a three-bedroom flat. My two sons will have their rooms and my wife and I will have one. Then it would be a decent life. I want you to write that the present two-bedroom flat is not of much help to us. Further, at least one of my sons should be sent to America to study as this was the dream of the daughter of the world," the father said.

"Don't you think that we need a better government and a better police administration in the national capital?" I asked, prepared to be insulted again.

I knew that I was crossing the limit. The job of a reporter is to collect information with the help of his or her subjects and other sources, file it and forget it. The life of a newspaper for most people is less than 30 minutes.

"The government is sincere. The police are also good. Such incidents can take place anywhere in the world." I could predict his tailor-made replies before asking him.

"Although I have asked you before I want to ask you again. Whom do you blame for what happened to your daughter?"

"She was not only my daughter," Badreshwar said in a loud voice. "I have said before that she was not my daughter alone. She was the daughter of the nation and the world. People sitting in faraway New York, want to hear the story of the daughter of India, daughter of the world."

"And I blame the criminals for whatever happened to her. The police caught them immediately. They will be punished for their acts anyway. The Prime Minister is concerned about everything. The politicians are united on this issue that women should be safe. They have taken measures for it. You can see that the police have been alert ever since the incident took place with the daughter of the world."

"The opposition says it is the failure of the government," I reminded him. He replied quickly, "There are good people in the Opposition. They are good people. They care for me. They care for the daughter of the world."

"OK. Fine. Thank you," I said.

But he started again before I could hang up.

"You must write about the three-bedroom house if you care about India and humanity. You should also ensure that my son goes to America. I can give you a long interview in the coming days and help you to become an editor of a newspaper," he promised without asking me if I needed his favour.

THIRTY-ONE

•••••••••••⋯⋯⋯⋯•••••••••

Several weeks passed. Then all of a sudden, one day I saw Badreshwar and Aniket on a news channel. They were addressing a news conference.

"She was not my daughter. She was the daughter of the nation and the world. Please don't call her a victim of gang rape. Call her a martyr," the father appealed to the media.

"The government was helpful and has given us a three-bedroom house. They have also started the process to send my son to America to study. But our demand to bestow on her the status of a martyr is still pending," he added.

The same day, I saw on a news channel that the boyfriend of the deceased arrived in court in a wheelchair. A reporter asked Kartik why he was not walking, and his father said, "He was beaten up by the rapists with an iron bar during the incident. He is still not able to walk."

Nobody can stop a centipede. But I am not a centipede. I can be stopped. I can be stopped by my emotions. I can also be stopped by one experience. A small kid can stop me from reaching my goal. I can change my route or delay my journey to shun someone I don't like or avoid facing.

THIRTY-TWO

●●●●●●●●●●●●●●●●●●●●●●●●

A month later, I read in a newspaper that Justice Sharma passed away. He had cancer, which he never disclosed to anybody. Sharma had already submitted his report to the government in which he had mentioned the poor conviction rate and the lack of will power of the government responsible for such incidents.

Normally, I wake up when the sun shone on my face. But there were dark clouds in the sky that morning.

I read in a newspaper – a single column news item – that the government had given Rs 50 lakh to Roshni's boyfriend for "showing bravery and trying his best to protect her".

I received a call the next day from a friend with whom I used to spend time in Paharganj. He wanted me to help an administrative officer suspended for dereliction of duty. My friend thought I could connect the officer with a politician who would help him out. I asked him to give my mobile number to the officer.

The officer called me within five minutes. He was shattered.

"I was suspended because I couldn't get the police officers in many stations in the city to extract sufficient money from local shop keepers and criminals to give to the family of the victim. However, every day, I used to collect money from the police stations for the family. But I didn't meet the target. So I was suspended," said the officer.

"I am an honest person in my personal life. My daughter is in a medical college and now I don't know how I will pay her fees." The officer spoke quickly without pausing to take a breath.

It was as if, after centuries, he found someone to pour out his heart. He continued, "I forced a market complex to open at midnight because the victim's brother wanted new shirts and pants and other items to travel abroad. Despite all this, I couldn't come up to the expectation of the family and my superiors."

"All I need from you is to arrange a meeting with the minister in charge of my department so that I can tell him my side of the story," he added.

I couldn't promise anything.

As I disconnected, I felt tired and exhausted as if I had been unwell for years. I felt like crying. I had no clarity of mind.

I have reported worse cases in the past. I've filed my copies and moved on.

After all, a story survives only a few minutes. Most people read the headlines only. Who doesn't know that most newspapers are waste in the afternoon?

Usually, I type my stories on a computer. Every journalist does so these days. But that morning I took out a sheet of A4 size paper and began to write.

Negotiating Delhi traffic is tough. That day, I started a bit early but reached the office before the afternoon meeting. I was restless. My editor arrived late and immediately called me. Normally we discuss the day's plan and scan the newspapers of the day.

Within seconds of entering his chamber, I handed my single-line letter to him. He read it attentively, looked at me twice and then said, "Fine. Accepted."

END